THE HOUSE ON MOON LAKE

—THE HOUSE—
ON
MOON LAKE

a novel by
FRANCESCA DURANTI

Translated from the Italian by
Stephen Sartarelli

COLLINS
8 Grafton Street London W1
1987

William Collins Sons & Co. Ltd
London · Glasgow · Sydney · Auckland
Toronto · Johannesburg

Originally published in Italy as *La casa sul lago della luna*
by Rizzoli Editore, Milano, 1984

This translation first published in the USA by Random House 1986
Published in Great Britain by William Collins 1987

BRITISH LIBRARY CATALOGUING IN PUBLICATION DATA

Duranti, Francesca
The house on moon lake.
I. Title   II. La casa sul lago della
luna. *English*
853'.914[F]   PQ4864.U68

ISBN 0-00-223156-5

Typeset in the United States of America

Made and Printed in Great Britain by
Robert Hartnoll (1985) Ltd, Bodmin, Cornwall

Contents

Part I

FULVIA

———— 1 ————

THAT MORNING Fabrizio finished his translation of the novel by Fontane. He typed the last line, pulled the sheet out of his typewriter and turned off the desk lamp. Resting his aching shoulders against the back of his chair, he allowed himself a few minutes of self-pity. He absorbed this emotion with great care, letting it permeate his whole being as in some kind of breathing exercise of the soul. *One, two*, an ill-paid job, *three, four*, and unhealthy, too.

Newly invigorated, he got up and opened the windows wide.

The April morning greeted the city's ungrateful inhabitants with a bright freshness for which the Milan climate is unjustly not renowned. A song of blackbirds, not yet drowned out by the roar of traffic, strayed from hidden green courtyards and onto the street, entering the open windows and spilling over into his study.

Fabrizio Garrone started toward his bedroom, turning his back to the sunlight. Fifteen years earlier, when leaving Genoa, he had taken with him only the books in his family library and a few other things he had saved. Everything else he had sold at auction. With the exception of the *Saint Jerome in his Study*, a small sixteenth-century Flemish panel-painting he had chosen only items of little value. Nevertheless, the costly atmosphere of the house in Genoa seemed to have followed those objects here, hovering about them like a crisper air, a warmer light reflected in the polished wood, a richer harmony of color in the torn fabric.

The ornate glass of the door leading to the foyer reflected his image surrounded by floral motifs; in the leafy frame and background of morning birdsongs it appeared to be that of a young faun frowning slightly.

Though Fabrizio was, in fact, thirty-eight years old, his gaunt face and fleshless limbs put him in the category of persons destined to turn back to dust without ever passing through the stage of life when increasing convexity lends the riper years an air of dignity.

He stood for some time leaning against the windowsill, staring at his own image without seeing it. He was thinking. Should he call Fulvia?

"Hello, love," he said out loud.

It did not sound right. He erased it with a brief cough.

"My dear," he tried again. That was more like it. The formal tone enabled him to reestablish contact while keeping a safe distance. "My dear, I've finished my Fontane! I'm going to start hunting for a new project right away. The first thing I'll do is go see Colombo. He called the other day to say that he had a novel for me. Döblin, I think it was."

Was this enough to give some purpose to his call, to fill it out, leaving no room for silent pauses? No, it wasn't. Every difficult moment between him and Fulvia invariably arose from her inflexible need for clarity; poorly hidden behind those pointless sentences so devoid of content, the words left unsaid would echo ruthlessly in all their obviousness and merely aggravate the situation. The night before, when Fulvia had stormed out of that very room hankering for a fight, she already knew everything: about Colombo, Döblin, and the fact that he was only a few pages away from finishing his translation. He had skillfully managed to avoid a direct confrontation;

it would be foolish to spoil everything now by acting on an ill-considered impulse.

He went back to looking out the window. The blinds of the building opposite were already raised. Earlier, when finishing his translation, he had resolved to deliver it right away to Mario, his neighbor across the way, who was also his editor for this particular job as well as his friend since childhood and an eater of sumptuous breakfasts. Fabrizio was thinking of dropping in on him for half an hour or so and sampling some of his piping-hot croissants, orange-blossom or rosemary honey, English marmalades and Chinese tea.

It occurred to him, however, that the wisest course of action was to reverse the morning's natural order. First, he would go to discuss the translation that had been offered him—he would go there on foot, make it a leisurely morning stroll. Of all the editors he knew, Colombo was the earliest riser, and his company's offices were rather far from the center of town. If he was not yet at work when Fabrizio arrived, no matter, he could wait. He would go up to Mario's later, when he got back; by then Fulvia would be there too, at work, just as on any other morning, and the three of them would have coffee together. Protected by Mario's presence, he could offhandedly drop the usual question—"So what you doing tonight, Fulvia? Are you coming by?"—at the last moment, before leaving. The fight in the making would be nipped in the bud: a clean, silent execution, without trial or sentence.

Colombo was already in his office when Fabrizio arrived and he received him at once, greeting him with a slight bow, which he quickly repressed. Some of the editors whom Fabrizio dealt with in his work would unintentionally assume a mildly deferential attitude in his presence, whereas others tended to intensify their natural rudeness; they all made him uncomfortable.

His secret dream was that Mario would become a publishing giant with the means to provide, all by himself, enough work so that he would not have to turn to anyone else to earn his living; but it was a dream that his friend clearly did not share.

Mario had left Genoa before Fabrizio, taking with him the modest savings that his parents had put aside for him during a life of hard work. He had become a publisher, sole owner and employee of a one-man business, making his home and office in the same four-room apartment. Within two years' time he had already made great strides toward realizing his ambitions: to live in reasonable comfort, to enjoy the respect of his peers, to know everyone and be known by everyone.

Thus when Fabrizio's father, emboldened by the death of his wife, embarked on a number of disastrous financial ventures, squandering the family fortune and then falling into a deep depression that was soon followed by his death, Mario was already in a position to help his friend by offering him work, finding him an apartment in Milan and introducing him to other publishers.

Since then Mario's business had continued to prosper, but—aside from his recent hiring of Fulvia—he had never dreamed of expanding, as he was convinced that the company's success was by and large due to its modest dimensions. And so Fabrizio, who made little more than one-tenth of his income by working for Mario, had to go knocking on other doors for the rest.

Earning a living is no easy task, he thought as he accepted the armchair that Colombo offered him.

"I've come about that translation you mentioned to me the other day. I would be free to do it now."

"Well, this is good news, Mr. Garrone," exclaimed Colombo. "Let me get it for you."

He began digging frantically through the manuscripts and books on the shelf behind his desk.

"You'll have to excuse me for just a moment. It was here, I put it here myself. . . Ah, here it is."

It was a very thick book. Fabrizio examined it with the expert eye of the translator paid by the page. Dense writing, little dialogue, few new paragraphs. Six hundred pages as solid as a black wall.

"Looks like a nice little grind."

"I won't deny it. Think it over, in any case. For this book I think I can get you a slightly higher rate than usual. Think about it; take the book home with you and look it over, at your convenience."

"All right. I'll let you know."

"Thank you. I appreciate it."

Colombo walked Fabrizio to the door, bent over him like a question mark or a curving vine, the deferential, solicitous arch rising up from his rounded shoulders and ending in a fleshy white face whose eyes seemed to pinch his rodentlike features too closely together. As he was saying good-bye, he tried momentarily to step out from the anonymity of their professional relationship and introduce a new vein of discussion.

"Have you seen the morning papers yet?"

Fabrizio had not seen them, nor had he any intention of seeing them. He had little concern for the present, convinced as he was that time would bury most of it: events, ideas, personalities. Why bother, then, trying to keep up with it all?

"No," he answered, "I haven't."

"There's an excellent article by Angelo Ceriani that you ought to look at. Very penetrating. Brilliant, I daresay."

Ceriani: the very name pierced Fabrizio's heart like a sharp blade. He loathed that mediocre *maître à penser* and secretly envied him his celebrity status in the culture industry. Without ever bothering much to learn why, he had a vague sense that Ceriani and others like him were responsible for having done away with his personal ideal of culture as something refined and a bit *démodé*, like all things that cannot be bought or acquired but are passed on naturally through family inheritance. He already knew everything about the article, as if he had actually read it—all the noisy, mindless splashing about on the surface, the useless froth; the success it would have, and all the subsequent talk. He could already see, plain as day, who would proclaim this success, and how they would discuss it, moving about in drawing rooms from one group to the next, drinks in hand, leaning confidentially over armchairs to listen to others speak, all of them privy to a perfect understanding—an understanding without object, based on nothing —in which they were all united, all except him, like a chorus that has rehearsed together a thousand times.

But Colombo's intelligent mouse-face beamed with enthusiasm and conviction, and Fabrizio didn't have the heart to disappoint him.

"I'll read it," he promised.

When he was back outside, the blade of vexation began to cut through his consciousness, penetrating deeper and deeper through tortuous channels that first began to intersect, then merged with one another, widening until they formed whole cavities of resentment: Ceriani's mystifications, and good old Colombo ready and willing to fall into their trap with all the others; the Döblin novel, tucked under his arm together with the Fontane translation, oppressively dragging him down with all the weight of a poorly paid labor; the usual dilemma of deciding what was the best approach to take with Fulvia, not only a few minutes from now, when he would see her at the office, but in the future as well—how to preserve the miraculous balance that he had managed to achieve in the last two years by keeping her as though poised on a single point, a point suitable to him but not to her, where she fretted and fidgeted dangerously, constantly threatening to bring them both tumbling down.

These and other thoughts had barely enough time to form in his mind before they become entangled with one another. He had always seen himself as the unhappy incarnation of all the historic defeats of the twentieth century, but usually this conviction was composed equally of irony and bitterness, which balanced each other out, so that the final result was fairly acceptable. Lately, however, the ratio was fast shifting in favor of bitterness, and all his lost battles seemed to be merging into one colossal defeat, to the point where he could no longer tell his victorious adversaries apart. He saw them the way many people see the Chinese—countless, menacing and all alike: rebellious women who questioned the rules of the game of love, two-bit thinkers who laid down the law of cultural ascendancy, drawing-room radicals who, with a couple of clichés, would peg him for a rightist, he who had voted for the left before revolutionary lingo became a sign of good taste; not to mention all the noisy motorcyclists, river-polluters, corrupt public officials, common criminals and political criminals, cutthroat greengrocers, rude and bewildered teenagers, rude and illiterate thirty-year-olds.

The triumphant horde teemed in the shadows, as in a childhood nightmare, and indeed, the feelings that wrung Fabrizio's heart—humiliation, a sense of injustice, impotence, rage—were those of a desperate, childlike distress.

Mario had only to take one look at Fabrizio to know that he was in a black mood. He knew him too well, and had known him too long, not to notice such things. Their childhood homes had stood on the same property, at once near to and far from each other, since the short distance that separated them, both horizontally and vertically, was the spatial symbol of a vast gulf on the social plane. Mario's house was the grounds-keeper's residence, and stood at the lowest level of the garden, which, like everything else in Liguria, sloped down, in over-lapping terraces, from the mountains to the sea. Fabrizio instead lived in the seventeenth-century master's villa, which had descended from heaven like a large pink cloud and settled on the highest terrace.

The heart of that house was the library on the second floor, where the august spirits of philologists, botanists and scholars still hovered in the air; they were all perched on branches a bit higher up the family tree, and some of them were even preserved, in image and name, for all to remember, in the pages of the Italian Encyclopedia.

That room emitted a dust of learning so fine and penetrating that it seemed to have settled in a solid layer in Fabrizio's consciousness, and in that of his sister, Teodora, as well—though she was possessed of a lust for life that he lacked —before either one of them had even learned to read. In fact, from the entire house, and from all the people and things within it—the wide, luminous vaulted ceiling, the precious objects, the light's reflection on the curved bellies of old chests of drawers, voices, gestures—there flowed a contagious sense of grace and beauty, as though from a miraculous fount, as when the blossoming wisteria rises to the top of a wall and spills fragrance and color onto the other side, like rain from the heavens, without stems, roots, props or any other visible source in the mortal world.

Mario was not excluded from that house. Perhaps Fabrizio's parents saw him as one of those humble animals—like cats, baby goats or chickens—that thoroughbreds are sometimes fond of.

And so the two boys grew up sharing their time, their thoughts and many material possessions as well; the last— garden, nursery, toys, books (and later on, the motorbike and car)—all belonged to Fabrizio. At some point, the weight of all these objects seemed to shift their friendship's center of gravity ever so slightly to the side of the richer boy, and Mario experienced a mysterious, imperceptible but unmistakable displacement of his focus of interests in the direction of Fabrizio's world. This spiritual undertow became even stronger when Mario had no reason to leave his own world below and ascend the garden, terrace by terrace, because there was no one waiting for him at the top. During those days of absence, which sometimes turned into weeks and even months, Mario, contrary to all the laws of logic, never felt separated from Fabrizio, even though his friend was far away; he felt he was following him, a silent, avid witness so close as to almost touch his friend, like a tiny, imperceptible though very attentive insect perched on that itinerant, more fortunate shoulder.

Thus, without ever leaving home, Mario visited distant cities, sailed to the Kornat islands on the yacht *Teodora*, rode horseback across Irish meadows, went mushroom-picking in Val Gardena. He became accustomed to living his friend's life with the same intensity as his own, showering him with constant attention, which Fabrizio came to rely on as the devotion of a caring, loyal guardian.

Fabrizio handed Mario the typescript.

"Here's your translation," he said gloomily. "And get a load of what Colombo just gave me."

He let the Döblin novel fall onto the desk with a dull thud.

"With a thing like that," he went on, "you can't even do a page an hour. My time will be worth less than a cleaning woman's."

Mario glanced at a few pages.

"More black than white," he admitted. "Let's go have a cup of coffee in the kitchen. Have you seen the piece by Ceriani yet?"

Ceriani again. New clouds darkened Fabrizio's face.

"You must be crazy," he said. "I never read the papers anyway, and you think I'm going to bother to keep up with that guy's drivel?" With long strides he followed his friend into the kitchen, the tails of his shapeless jacket flapping over his dark blue sweater. Whether dressed in the old Caraceni suits of the opulent years or in simple corduroy jeans, he was always immediately recognizable as a "rare specimen"—like the furniture, the carpets, the paintings in whose midst he had grown up.

"You, I suppose, are a fan of that hack," he continued.

It was the truth, but Mario could not quite own up to it. His

11

opinions, like his clothes, always seemed, by comparison, less elegant than Fabrizio's, even when the former were much sounder and the latter more expensive.

"Bah. I'm no fan of his. I read everything; I like to know what's going on. But now finish your coffee and be off. I've got a lot to do this morning."

"Where's Fulvia?"

"Gone to the printer. I don't know when she'll be back."

He walked Fabrizio to the door.

"See you soon," he said.

—— 2 ——

FABRIZIO STEPPED OUT OF THE DOORWAY, walked to the end of the street, then turned left, continuing for another several hundred meters until he reached the park. He sifted through his bad mood, trying to unravel it, to break it down into its prime factors.

First of all Fulvia. Or women as a whole, just to proceed, in analytical fashion, from the general to the particular. Nothing but trouble, right from the start. The torment he suffered at sixteen, on the occasion of Teodora's eighteenth birthday party. They all seemed as happy as could be that night. Airy, fragrant creatures filled the rooms downstairs like flowers in an overflowing basket, spilling over through the French windows in colorful streams, into the garden moonlight.

Teodora, proud and willful with her liberated notions and her whimsical clothes, was the queen of that party, which was in her honor, just as she was queen of every other party she attended. She knew how to strike the perfect balance between conformity and originality; in fact, her transgressions of the laws of social convention not only did not put her outside or even at the fringe of the magic circle, they actually led her to the very center through general acclaim, making her the object of a curiosity that bordered on gossip, an amazement that bordered on scandal, an admiration that bordered on envy.

Mario, as a friend of the birthday girl's brother, divided his time between the pleasure of flirting with the pretty girls and the duty of dancing with the homely ones; but to see him so eager and attentive one would have thought that he enjoyed the duty—a sign of his privileged status in that house, as almost an adopted son—more than the pleasure.

Fabrizio neither danced with the homely girls nor flirted with the pretty ones. He sat off in a corner, tongue-tied by a vague uneasiness and unable to accept his silence. He hated himself for being so different from the others, and hated the others even more for being so different from him. He ended his misery by running and hiding in the library.

At that age it already seemed impossible for him to establish relationships with the living as deep and gratifying as those he could have with the dead, especially the long dead. He could hear the masters speak to him through their books, always finding in their words a message meant only for him—whether encouragement, praise or sometimes just a discreet wink, as if to say: "You and I understand each other perfectly."

He had by then already experienced his first stirrings of passion, kindled in him by his mathematics teacher, the dread Miss Ferzetti.

She was a tiny woman in her middle years. Her hair was dyed a dull, flat yellow devoid of sheen, and this color seemed to hold together, all by itself—without the help of nets or hairpins—her entire head of hair, creating a single, solid mass that absorbed all stray or rebellious strands. Her face had no distinguishing features and was yellow as well, though slightly lighter in tone. Even in its softer shades, this color still maintained its unifying power; nothing—not a gleam of irony or the hint of a smile—ever stirred within or escaped from that compact prison of yellow.

Her small, slight body was always wrapped in a black satin frock; her shoes were dark with low heels, and her slender ankles rose up from the very center of her feet, equidistant from heels and toes. Miss Ferzetti's feet were the seal of her authority, the symbol of her knowledge, the center of her equilibrium; they completed her geometrical symmetry, making it impossible to speak, in her regard, of a front or a back. She was rigid, abstract, bifrontal.

One morning, while standing at the blackboard trying to solve an equation, Fabrizio became momentarily distracted. The rhythm of numbers charmed him as much as the magic of words; he did not suffer from that singular incompetence in math that students who are "good in Italian" or "good in English" often seem to take pleasure in. But he was fifteen years old and growing too fast, and at times—such as that very moment—he felt as though all his blood had drained off into a crack in the floor, leaving him empty-headed and weak in the knees.

The equation had swollen all out of proportion beneath his piece of chalk, and Fabrizio, like an inexperienced sheepdog overwhelmed by his flock, suddenly found himself unable to bring that multitude of incomprehensible signs back under control.

Miss Ferzetti allowed him a few seconds to work it out by himself; then she got up from her desk, took the chalk and began to cross out the equation's opposite terms with sharp, decisive little strokes all identical in length and slant.

"Pay attention, Garrone. This one and this one: out. These other two: out. It's getting clearer now, isn't it? See, there's nothing to be afraid of. Away with this and this."

She continued crossing numbers out, then began to mark the similar terms. Fabrizio was quite a bit taller than she and had written out the equation at the very top of the blackboard, right beneath the frame. In order to reach that high, Miss Ferzetti had to extend her arm as far is it would go, pulling her black dress upward in the process and exposing, beneath the hem, a wide strip of pink slip—about an inch of lace, and right above it a fold, a flounce. Fabrizio didn't quite know what it was called as he stood in rapt attention, ravenously studying that little tidbit of unexpected intimacy. It was a piece of work that Miss Ferzetti—though it seemed out of character—had done with her own hands, shortening the garment to make it fit her tiny proportions, and not denying herself the coquettish extravagance of lace.

The hand-sewn stitches—little dots of earnest ineptitude—were plainly visible; the pink lace, however, was unmarred and delicately brushed against her leg, overshadowed by the black satin curtain poised to fall back down at any moment over that precious secret.

Fabrizio, as of that moment, plunged into an extended amorous swoon. Every morning he would gaze long at Miss Ferzetti, later bringing home with him the warmth and fragrance of her secret femininity, which would fill his room and mix with the tepid spring air, laden with pollen, that came in through the open windows.

A feminine figure came up behind him on the path, walked beside him a few seconds—just long enough to chase away his ghosts—then passed him. A solid girl dressed in green, her left ear exposed all the way to the nape of her neck, her right ear covered by a mass of shiny black curls. Waves of carbon monoxide announced, just a few steps away, the end of the park and the beginning of the real city. The real girl headed toward the real city. Fabrizio remembered some lines of Catullus: "Scortillum, ut mihi tum repente visum est, non sane illepidum neque invenustum," that is, "A little strumpet, as she suddenly appeared before me, was not without spirit and grace." That girl was a little strumpet, no doubt, going her merry way, carefree and fearless.

And braless. Fabrizio did not find this in any way seductive. On the contrary, he liked ties and straps, bands that dug furrows into the flesh. Girls without bras undressed too casually for his tastes, made it too obvious that they were in control of the situation. To release a woman from all her secret

hooks, especially when they were a bit shabby and pathetic—
that was something else. Women of that kind, when the
moment arrived, would hesitate a long time, pausing as if to
say "Vorrei e non vorrei"; they would blush; sometimes they
would even try awkwardly to defend themselves. Even if they
—like all the rest—did not possess the charm of modesty (that
wonderful aphrodisiac that gave one the illusion of stepping
with coarse, muddy boots into an immaculate sanctuary), at
least they produced something which was similar and almost
as exciting when combined with their embarrassment over
their undergarments.

The strumpet in green—smooth-skinned, braless and
shameless—wiggled around the corner, plunging, together
with Teodora's girlfriends, Miss Ferzetti, Fulvia and Döblin,
back into the teeming depths of Fabrizio's vague anxieties.

At the edge of the park there was a bookstall selling old
and used editions. Fabrizio stopped to have a look, and upon
seeing some of the names—Ferdinando Martini, Viani, Fucini,
Pea—he imagined their owner to have been an old Tuscan
gentleman very fond of his native region who had perhaps
died in exile, given that his library was now up for sale in
Milan. Probably a landowner—with vineyards, olive groves
and game preserves in the splendid, breathtaking countryside
between Volterra and Siena; a lean man who still wore on old-
fashioned orange Casentino overcoat trimmed with domestic
fox fur, eccentric and perhaps a bit of a fascist, but not wicked.
Or else a provincial lawyer (from Lucca? Pisa?) whose second
love, after his native Tuscany, seemed to be philology, since
the likes of Comparetti, De Robertis and Pasquali were mixed
and at times stuck together with the Tuscan authors, having
probably lived beside them a long time in a dark wooden,
pseudo-Renaissance bookcase. They were all old books: no
doubt this lawyer too (or the landowner with the Casentino
overcoat) had begun one day to feel a certain irritation at what
was finding its way into print. Or else one of his heirs (a

daughter, and an upper-class idiot—white sofas, huge stainless steel ashtrays, cane sugar with gilt granules in her coffee) had decided to keep the more "interesting" things—the latest purchases—and get rid of all the other rubbish.

Fabrizio flipped through the old gentleman's books; finally he bought a small collection of essays by Giorgio Pasquali. It was an old provincial edition, which he liked for its tasteful simplicity; he didn't really expect it to contain anything that had not been reprinted in later collections.

When he returned to the park and sat down on a bench to peruse the book more closely, he was surprised to find in it an essay that he had never seen before.

It was an article printed in 1913 on the occasion of a stage premiere. At one point, while discussing the obtuseness and excessive caution of certain impresarios, the author wrote:

> That, on the other hand, is just the way things are these days, even outside the theater. For example, I recently suggested to five different publishers that I translate *Das Haus am Mondsee* by Fritz Oberhofer, a novel that came into my hands purely by chance, as only one hundred copies of it had been privately printed, in Vienna. Every one of them turned it down because the book, whose author is totally unknown even in his native Austria, would not be a guaranteed success. I, however, am perfectly confident that it would take the public by storm, because of the profound, delicately conceived love affair between the two protagonists. The subtle ambiguities and contradictions that hide behind their emotions and, in a sense, sustain them are part of an original, successful invention that is both surprising and convincing.

Pasquali then left Fritz Oberhofer and his *House on Moon Lake* and returned to his previous argument.

Fabrizio reread the last sentence, or rather gazed at it as he might a class photo that brought back memories of some last day at school. There was nothing conclusive about it, nothing destined to go down in history. The words had come together for only a moment, just long enough to be set down on the page, after which they each went their separate ways, like students in summer. The dust that collects on final statements would never fall on those subtle, ambiguous lines, which meant that they could, at any moment—perhaps an April morning in the park, under the trees—spring back to life, ringing with the resonance of a new and uncorrupted truth.

Fabrizio got up from the bench and began to pace back and forth, unable to contain his excitement. He sat back down to reread the passage. A Viennese novelist of the most fashionable period who specialized in subtleties of love. A writer capable of "original, successful invention that is both surprising and convincing." And what was this, if not poetry? A complete unknown.

Of that much Fabrizio was certain. "If *I've* never heard of you," he thought with justifiable conceit, "then nobody has." A complete unknown. A great writer. A great *Viennese* writer.

Just when the wall of estrangement that separated him from others seemed to have surrounded him completely, lo and behold, a crack had suddenly appeared, affording him a chance to crawl through to the other side, to that happy world where people decanted the fluid transparence of their humanity into solid vessels. Fritz Oberhofer would make him a Germanist: every title, or almost every title, that ended in *-ist* conferred an unassailable status on its bearer, ensured his place within a given framework, gave him a recognizable physiognomy.

There was a world of difference between the Germanist and the eclectic, multilingual man of culture whose literary background *included* a knowledge of German literature, the respected translator who worked from the German, *among other things*. This vast difference could be measured just by considering the inordinate number of words needed to define—and only roughly at that—the latter category. By contrast, one had only to say "Germanist," a single word, terse as the snap of a whip, and the credentials came rolling out automatically, like a red carpet at the feet of some high dignitary.

It was now past noon and the park was already deserted. A blackbird scratched about in the bushes. "A crack in the wall," murmured Fabrizio.

Not a welcoming open door; just an oversight. To take full advantage of the opportunity, he would have to operate quietly and in secret.

He immediately thought of Mario as the publisher of his discovery, but at the same time felt gripped by a new distrust. Or rather, it was that his usual distrust had burst its banks and engulfed the only person it had spared until that moment. Mario would, eventually, get to publish the book and share in its success; but first Fabrizio had to look into the matter on his own.

He passed in front of his friend's house without stopping and ran and shut himself up in his apartment.

—————— 3 ——————

STANDING AT THE TOP of a ladder in his spacious, silent study, Fabrizio put back the last of the volumes he had just consulted. He turned around to look from above at his room, his books, his desk. Though there had been no doubt in his mind, only now that he had confirmed his hunch did it seem that the adventure had really begun; the essay containing the reference to Fritz Oberhofer was not included in the more recent reprints of the works of Giorgio Pasquali; hence it was highly unlikely that some other scholar might already, at that moment, be on the trail of the unknown Austrian's novel; the task, then, was his.

It was still a few minutes before one; Helga, the librarian at the Goethe Institute, had probably not gone for lunch yet. He climbed down from the ladder, went to the phone and dialed her number.

As always, she was happy to hear his voice. German women usually went wild over him, so dark and lean; they found him very *temperamentvoll*.

"Oberhofer, you said?"

"Yes, Oberhofer."

"No, there's nothing. Who is he?"

"Oh, nobody. Probably just an error of transcription. Thanks. Take care now."

This, too, he had expected. A hundred copies printed for private circulation, surely at the author's expense; the author no doubt a dilettante to whom no one had paid any attention; a few copies given away to friends, as Christmas gifts, then put away in some far corner and forgotten, lost . . .

Das Haus am Mondsee had disappeared, and no one knew the first thing about Fritz Oberhofer. Fabrizio could look for the book in peace.

He would be the first to find it.

He felt as if the thoughts he was forming were not his own, but were invading him from within, in waves, like the light of a flashing sign entering a dark room through an open window.

But what if the librarian at the Goethe Institute was to get curious? What if she decided to do some investigation on her own? What if she started scattering the name of Fritz Oberhofer to the four winds?

He had to act fast and in secret. He dared not utter that name again until he had been to the National Library of Vienna. The trip would be expensive, but is was essential that he stay in Vienna as long as was needed to find not only the book he was looking for and information on the author's life but also any other novels he might have written. Mario had paid him in advance for the translation of the Fontane novel, but most of the money had already gone to pay the rent on his apartment. Fabrizio emptied his wallet, checked his bankbook and decided that everything he had would not be enough to finance the undertaking.

Of course, the most logical solution to his problem would have been Mario. He was his friend, he had helped him before. Fabrizio was already looking forward to the pleasure he would derive from sharing his treasure with him, as soon as he could get his hands on it. But was it wise to go and tell him everything now, and then ask him to pay for the trip?

It was possible that Mario would act just like Giorgio Pasquali's five publishers and turn down the offer; but that was not the real problem. The doubt that was troubling Fabrizio was: Would he take Fritz Oberhofer away from him? If Mario was confident that *Das Haus am Mondee* could be a winning card, would he run the risk of letting Fabrizio play it?

Fabrizio had no illusions as to which of the two would find the book first if they were both to set out looking for it. Their mutual esteem was based on a kind of unwritten pact that assigned to each his own spheres of influence, before which the other would always bow down. In anything that required the least bit of initiative, speed and practicality, Fabrizio would never have dreamed of competing with Mario. Indeed, if Mario decided to take *Das Haus am Mondsee* away from him, he would already have a seat reserved on a flight to Vienna, a room waiting for him at the Sacher and an appointment set up with the director of the National Library of Vienna before Fabrizio had finished asking him for the money; and while Fabrizio was still working out his travel plans, his friend would already be back in Milan with the book, ready to place the bomb in illustrious hands to make it explode with as much noise as possible.

Mario could do so if he wanted to; of that there was no doubt. Fabrizio's aristocratic ineptitude and Mario's plebeian knack for business were roles that were never questioned.

But would he ever want to do such a thing? Fabrizio thought he would. It was an unfair, ungrateful thought, but he no longer bore responsibility for the thoughts that had swept him away that morning, for those few hours of his life had gathered up his inner ghosts like the Sargasso Sea, which had once brought together all the ocean's algae (or eels?) in a single area, and now, it seemed, collected all the garbage and plastic floating on our dying seas.

These same ghosts would tear him away from his fellow creatures during the events that followed, imprisoning him in a solitary nightmare where the real, the possible and the imaginary played games that followed strange and dangerous rules.

Of all these ghosts, the one that haunted him the most was the desperate feeling of exclusion—he on one side of the glass, everyone else on the other, gathered together as though in an aquarium, suspended in a different, hostile element. Sure, he was considered a good translator; but did anyone give him credit for his training, taste and talent as a man of letters? Maybe Mario, he thought; but—he wondered simultaneously —would he, his friend, have the courage to assign a winning horse to a jockey whom everyone thought mediocre?

How, he asked himself bitterly, could Mario ever expect the public to have any interest in an author discovered by Fabrizio Garrone when Fabrizio Garrone himself did not exist, or existed only in transparent form, a subject without predicate, an image without shape?

Was it possible that Mario had not yet recognized Fabrizio's overwhelming propensity for failure, even after having seen him behave like an utter fool, time and time again, when faced with that most idiotic of tests, the social occasion? But here Fabrizio's pride rebelled for a moment. Better to be a fool in those circumstances than to be like the rest. There was a little song that Mademoiselle Adine used to sing to him when he was a child, a song that contained the Supreme Law of Conversation reigning in all the drawing rooms of the cultured Milanese bourgeoisie:

> Quand une sardine
> rencontre une autre sardine
> qu'est-ce qu'elles debinent
> l'histoire d'une autre sardine.
>
> Quand un gendarme
> rencontre un autre gendarme
> qu'est-ce qui les charme
> des histoires de gendarmes.*

* When a sardine
  meets another sardine

Fabrizio was neither a sardine nor a gendarme. He was not an editor of any paper, nor did he belong to the Italian Psychoanalytic Association. He did not write essays on love and did not design silverware, armchairs or ashtrays. He did not really belong to that larger, nameless confraternity which to those on the outside seemed as specific and rigid as a professional society and as scornful and closed as a social caste, but whose requirements for membership were extremely difficult to define and tended to blur and overlap one another—money, education, success, talent, refinement, good looks—though none of these were really necessary and none of them really enough, so that in the end, the inquiring mind became discouraged and fell back on the mystical conclusion that the only requirement for membership was membership itself and membership alone. He was not part of any professional organization, since there were no such things as "translators' circles," as far as he knew; and even if such sorry coteries did exist, he would flee them like the plague. What else was left for him but to listen to the shoptalk of the "others," never taking part except to moan from time to time?

"But then, why do you bother with any of it?" he asked himself. Why indeed could he never say no, like the silly girl who rushes off to the ball every time, hoping to dance with the prince?

The horror of those parties! And the shame of being there, and of knowing that he would go every time he was invited anew—it was an utter mystery why they kept inviting him and why he was always so ready to accept. All that chatter, aside from being alien to him, seemed quite boring; yet the

---

What's their routine
but talk of another sardine.

When a gendarme
meets another gendarme
What is certain to charm
is a tale of gendarmes.

tone of the words pronounced—the stress and cadence, the expressions on people's faces, their gestures—always demanded a cheerful response. To refuse it would be like refusing an outstretched hand. Whether out of human decency, or else for fear of no longer being asked to those dreadful ceremonies, one had no choice but to twist one's face into a smile, a grimace, and bear it to the bitter end. It was tough as a horse's bit and became heavier and more painful to wear as the hours passed; but the hours did pass, thank God, until, once outside the door, he could finally relax his face, letting the smirk spill down from his mouth, over his chin, throat and finally his chest, where it rolled into many overlapping folds like a collar of uncooked dough. He was a lost cause, doomed never to know success, social or otherwise. How could anyone possibly have any faith in him?

There was nothing left to do but to pay his own way to Vienna, travel expenses and hotel room, for as long a period as was needed; to bring the book home, once he had found it, and to set about translating it, at the risk of wasting not only money but endless days of work. Indeed, what guarantee was there that Mario, once presented with the finished product, would want to publish it?

Living from hand to mouth, without even the slightest margin of security, was repugnant to him. Though he had never taken the trouble to set anything aside, he was careful never to let things get out of control. His bank account rarely exceeded a million lire at any one time, but then he never let it dip below three hundred thousand either. Now he suddenly felt himself recoiling like a frightened animal from the prospect of an adventure that he could not afford even if he spent every lira he had.

Could he have success within reach and fail to seize it? Quite easily, he told himself bitterly, and went to open the door, as the bell had just rung.

—————— 4 ——————

FULVIA STOOD wide-eyed at the door, purse slung over her left shoulder, her right arm blossoming into a blue plastic bag like a gigantic overturned bellflower. She hadn't felt like going out alone to eat, she said, and since she had to be back at the office for a two-thirty appointment, she didn't have enough time to go back home.

"I bought some things at the rotisserie," she added, "but if you're busy I'll go back and eat with Mario."

"You're just in time," he said. "I was about to boil myself an egg. Come in, I'm glad you came." The girl made for the kitchen. According to Fabrizio's classification, Fulvia, though thirty-five years old, belonged to the category of "strumpet," and not only because she didn't wear a bra.

It was her strong and confident gait, the sign of a profound independence though uncushioned by the rubber soles of the first feminists; it was the bold firmness of her limbs, the sheen of her hair; it was the unfailing appropriateness of her gestures —these qualities and others had led to Fabrizio's classification of her.

Fulvia put the plastic bag on the table.

"I forgot to buy wine," she said. "If you don't have any, I'll run out and get some."

"I've got a nice cold bottle of white in the fridge."

"Well, open it then. This stuff's ready to eat."

She unwrapped the packages of food and set the table with her usual confident gestures, lightly touching each object with a familiarity that put everything in its proper place, squaring the angles and reestablishing a sense of symmetry. Fabrizio welcomed her calm, steady reliability with gratitude, knowing he could entrust his weary mind to her care without having to reveal his doubts or their cause, but setting both aside for a while like a child before a benign authority that he knows is willing—if necessary—to look out for him.

They had met two years earlier, at a dinner at the house of friends. They had gone out a few times together; then one day she invited him to come spend the Saint Ambrose holiday weekend at her father's house in Valtellina.

As he always did when something impressed or upset him, Fabrizio, as soon as he got back to Milan, rushed to Mario's with a report. Every little thing about his visit had charmed him: the aroma of the kitchen; the living room and its standard Cantù furniture; the workshop where Fulvia's father made casks, tubs and barrels, assisted by his son and two workmen; the linen sheets in which he had slept.

He leaned back in the armchair as he related all this to his friend, smiling broadly and casting an occasional glance upward as if to gaze upon ineffable sights, repeating: "Extraordinary, I tell you, unbelievable."

Mario was always one to search tirelessly for the meaning of things, but when the thing in question involved Fabrizio, it also reawakened his old sense of having the responsibility— and the right—to look after his friend. So, without asking Fabrizio any questions—since he spoke without prompting— Mario followed him attentively, trying to single out from the mist of that torrent of adjectives something solid on which to base his own understanding. He knew his friend too well to believe he had been infected, a few years late, by the bombast that the simple, rural life had inspired in so many others; and he was so close to being right that when the long-awaited answer finally came out, he nearly started laughing, for the thing that had so happily solidified Fabrizio's budding affections for Fulvia and extended them to the rest of her family was a question of money, a cold, hard element known to unleash all sorts of malfeasance in people, but which certainly has the merit of being infertile ground for bombast.

It seemed that Adelmo Basso, the cooper, had filled a very large order for a local winemaker, and this fellow, a well-known troublemaker, kept finding excuses for not paying, and had been dragging his feet for quite some time.

"You should have seen them," said Fabrizio. "On Sunday afternoon all four of them—Adelmo, his son and the two workmen—put on their finest clothes and set off marching, just like an army: big, strong, wooden and enveloped in that smell of sawdust that never leaves them; they went straight to this client's house, to settle the matter once and for all. They made no threats; they didn't even raise their voices. They simply formed a line in front of him, calm and unruffled, never batting an eyelid. And he paid up. When they got back home they all got drunk, including me."

"In short," said Mario, "you fell in love with the whole family after seeing them recover a debt."

Fabrizio was silent a moment, absorbed in thought.

"Yes, something like that," he said finally. "I don't quite know why, but I think you just might be right."

Mario, for his part, knew why; he had known it from the moment he pictured Fabrizio catching a glimpse of the inner workings of a well-ordered mind, with its two columns—debits and credits—neatly logged in and lined up next to each other. He seemed, on the other hand, to have gained for the first time a sense of the vast, deep-rooted confusion that

29

reigned in his friend's inner ledger; he realized that his give and take, his requests and denials, were motivated not nearly so much by heartfelt conviction as by whimsical feelings and resentments bolstered by subtleties of logic that he himself didn't believe in. In Fulvia he must have recognized and immediately come to love the sign of a higher order of reliability; like a prince in a fable, he had followed the strange maiden to her father's abode and there, above the tall portal, he had seen the escutcheon with its inscribed motto, the proof of her lineage.

Fabrizio had to introduce her to his friend right away. The meeting took place at Mario's house. An excellent meal was prepared, the dinner table set in the living room with Mario's best tablecloth. The vases were filled with flowers, the refrigerator stocked with Rhine wines; it was to be an official introduction of friends, and Mario had taken it all very seriously.

As soon as Mario laid eyes on Fulvia he thought she was the most beautiful woman he had ever seen, though he realized, in forming this opinion, that her charm was strictly personal, for there was nothing particularly striking about her, just a soft harmony of sweet, warm colors—a blend of caramel, honey and ripe peach. She was not very tall, but her firm, slender body seemed to be that of a woman who carried her own suitcases and was capable of fixing a short circuit. Her placid smile was neither coy nor frivolous; she emanated peace, strength and health.

Mario sat her down on the sofa and immediately began to fuss over her, offering her a bowl of olives, asking her if she wanted him to put on a record, offering her cigarettes, tinkering with the lighting and adjusting the windows, then back to the olives, cigarettes and aperitifs.

Fabrizio also put on a performance, but in a different role from Mario; he was not the solicitous host but the brilliant conversationalist, author of witticisms and paradoxes.

She divided her attention between the two of them, never

missing a beat; she smiled, ate a few olives, drank a glass of white wine. She didn't talk much, but the few things she did say were said with a minimum of syllables and pauses, using compact words which contained a great deal of substance, intelligence and spirit, like bright little nuggets very high in specific density.

At one point Mario left Fulvia and Fabrizio sitting next to each other to go into the kitchen and fetch the dinner, and it was like leaving behind a golden tropical beach gently washed by the carpet's blue waves.

When, after a series of hasty, careless movements, he suddenly found himself with a red-hot frying pan in his right hand, a bottle of white in his left and his entire stock of frozen foods crashing down on top of him from the open freezer, Fulvia miraculously appeared at his side. Her hands protected by a dishcloth, she relieved him of the frying pan and wine, taking everything to its proper place on the dinner table, then put all the frozen foods back in the freezer in stable geometric piles before Mario had even recovered from his momentary confusion. He realized this was not a feat of any major proportion, and yet the way she had carried it out, with movements which were swift without being fussy and an imperturbable Olympian smile, seemed to him a sign of her benign, providential nature. He thought of her as more than beautiful, strong, sweet, intelligent and witty; yet he always denied, even to himself, that he had fallen in love with her that first evening, perhaps to rule out in his own mind the possibility that Fulvia had set an old, familiar mechanism in motion again, joining ranks with Fabrizio's tricycle and nursery, tea with scones, his library, his Alfa Romeo.

Yet the images of that first encounter had always remained vivid in his memory, like those of an unforgettable occasion, and what could be more unforgettable than a *coup de foudre*?

And of all those images—the golden colors, the calm sweetness of her voice—the one he remembered best was the charm of Fulvia's profile; and what is a profile if not the face of someone looking at someone else?

But whatever the precise moment of their genesis or the secret reason for their existence, the fact was that Mario did not refrain from cultivating his feelings for Fulvia, especially since he soon realized that things between her and Fabrizio were not going well enough to convince him that, motivated by the loftiest of principles, he should take a chivalrous step back and abandon all hope.

The thing that was not going so well was Fabrizio, who was hopelessly torn between contradictory feelings: the more his love for Fulvia grew and deepened, the more it frightened him, as though it were a fate for which he was not prepared.

She on the other hand saw no threat in what Mario, with a bachelor's wariness, had once termed "the test of two," something which Fabrizio, with his much deeper, darker fear, had no name for and could not even conceive. She had already faced the "test" before, in fact, when she married at the age of twenty. But then her husband suddenly died in an automobile accident, and she had to shed many tears, work till she dropped and wait years and years before the clot of grief that weighed so heavily on her chest finally stopped seeming a permanent obstruction and began to break down, soon rejoining her regular circulation and letting all her other feelings flow freely again.

For several years she had been unable to accept a new love. But when she met Fabrizio, life as a twosome again became, just as before, a situation she embraced quite naturally. She was made for it; she knew the rules of the game and could play it without effort.

Fabrizio, on the other hand, couldn't let himself go; he was incapable of admitting another person into that secret recess, off-limits to friends and siblings, where love resides. But neither did he walk away from love. He would have liked to be able simply to linger at love's doorstep, without ever going forward or backward; but in order to keep things as they were, he felt he had to minimize their reality, to thwart their chances for finding expression in words or progressing with time. He was prepared to resort to any means necessary—phony excuses, feigned illness, genuine rudeness—to keep his meetings with Fulvia, whom he saw every day, with rare exception, in a state of permanent incoherence in which it was impossible to discern any sort of pattern or sequence. And in this resolve he showed great powers of obstruction, an uncanny ability to hinder, stifle, deny and ignore.

This negative power, which took the joy and spontaneity out of his relationship with Fulvia, was nevertheless the very thing that, by relegating their rapport to a limbo of indeterminacy and chance and thus stripping it of most of the thorns that Fabrizio found so threatening, made it perfectly and eternally acceptable to him.

It was Fulvia who now and then got fed up with it all. Occasionally, when Fabrizio was at the height of his vagueness, Fulvia would seem to withdraw silently from her commitment. She would go on seeing him, sometimes even spending the night with him, but she did not deprive herself of other encounters, other affairs. Certain men seem to have a nose for mistreated women and know exactly when to appear on the scene; or perhaps it was just that Fulvia always kept a few spare suitors on ice for such occasions. Whatever the case—it's a small world, and Milan is a small town—on a number of occasions even Mario became aware that suddenly it was Fulvia who was being vague, leaving all her plans up in the air. But what he noticed most of all was that while Fabrizio resorted to such behavior to preserve some semblance of hypothetical freedom for himself which he never took advantage of, Fulvia treated herself to genuine, tangible amusements.

This discovery aroused ambivalent feelings in Mario. On the one hand, he could not rid himself of the conventional idea that an affair was supposed to be more erotically exciting than a long-standing relationship, and as a result these flings made him much more jealous than did any thought of Fulvia in Fabrizio's arms. In fact, since he had managed successfully to banish such thoughts from his mind, it was only the "others" who made him feel jealous, struck him to the quick of his emotions and wounded his pride.

On the other hand, since he was convinced that her transgressions would, in the long run, undermine her relationship with Fabrizio, he derived a painful, bitter satisfaction from them, not unlike that which his father said he had felt, along with so many other Italians, during the Allied bombings.

He was wrong, however, because Fulvia's unfaithfulness did not have the same effect as the destruction of bridges and railways, which helped bring Fascism and the war to an end. On the contrary, her affairs actually helped preserve the stability of their relationship. On the one hand, they secretly reassured Fabrizio, while on the other they quite visibly alarmed him, penetrating deep into his consciousness and stirring up contradictory feelings which were nevertheless dominated by a strange sense of admiration for and solidarity with Fulvia; it was as though he could step outside himself and feel delighted with Fulvia for having taught that unworthy lover of hers a lesson. These episodes themselves led to the use of the term "strumpet," which in the secret language of their love became an affectionate, playful pet name. When things got to this point, Fabrizio's behavior would begin to show signs of a certain progress, however slow, toward maturity, while Fulvia, for her part, would feel enough guilt to make herself take an extra dose of tolerance—just to keep her impeccable inner ledger balanced—for the inevitable difficulty of loving a man like the one she had chosen.

There were no ambiguities, second thoughts or ulterior motives among the practical considerations that prompted Mario to suggest that Fulvia leave her modest position with a large publisher to come and work with him. His company was no longer so small that he could keep managing it alone, but neither was it large enough to permit a real division of duties according to specialization. He actually needed someone like Fulvia, someone versatile and down-to-earth, able and willing to play all roles, from editor to messenger to publicist. Fulvia, while not a bookworm, was quite well-read; she had a highly presentable appearance (too presentable, according to Fabrizio, who accused both her and Mario of that most inelegant of foibles, taking one's clothes too seriously); and most important, she had, hiding beneath that smooth exterior, the fibre of the Bassos, a family of hard, tireless workers.

Yet there were reasons of a different nature behind Mario's decision, and these were fraught with conflict. Mario told himself that all he had done was make a noble gesture of friendship toward Fulvia, designed to help her put her tortuous relationship with Fabrizio back in order and give her a more solid, official position—making her almost one of the family, not to mention bringing her geographically closer to her lover for many hours a day.

But he did not hide from himself the fact that his maneuver might have the opposite effect and bring on the end of their shaky love. He might even have been secretly counting on this, hoping to worm his way into taking Fabrizio's place. "After all," he thought, "*noblesse oblige. He is a gentleman, isn't he? If he has to lose, he'll know how to lose gracefully.*"

5

FABRIZIO GAZED AT FULVIA, in her English wool and Florentine leather, as she set the kitchen table. When she was around, everything became clear again—the whole web of events, characters and relationships became as simple as a nursery rhyme, as plain as a string of paper dolls cut out with a few snips of the scissors. There were the bad guys—the vain, indifferent society, the debased culture; the good guys—the disillusioned intellectual and his wise, loyal girlfriend; and the fairy godmother—Giorgio Pasquali, who from the beyond had provided the treasure map. And there was Mario, the generous, trusty friend. "How," thought Fabrizio, "could I ever have doubted him?"

The ghosts seemed ready to fall back in line. Fabrizio decided that later, after Fulvia had gone and he had given a bit more thought to the matter, he would go see Mario, to talk to him about Fritz Oberhofer, so they could decide together what to do.

For the time being he thought it best not to mention any of this to Fulvia, preferring to set his worries temporarily aside.

"I tried to call you about an hour ago," she said. "Mario wanted to know when I intend to take my vacation."

"I was taking a walk in the park. Your vacation?"

"What he really wants to know is when he can go on vacation himself. We can't close up shop and go away at the same time, except during the short August holidays. You know what he's like; he likes to arrange everything ahead of time."

Fabrizio let out a forced little laugh.

"No, he's certainly not the type to decide things at the last minute—sleeping bag, makeshift bed on a pool table and that sort of thing. The boy needs time if he's going to set up something fancy for himself. . . ." He piled words on top of one another like stones for a barricade. "Just imagine, he has succeeded in getting his name on the VIP list of BEA, Pan American and who knows what else—"

Fulvia interrupted him. "Just listen for a moment."

But he went on: "That way, while he's waiting for the plane they stick him in a little room all his own, or maybe with a few other VIPs; they give him a telephone, so he can make a hundred useless phone calls, and then they bring him champagne, which of course he hates but drinks anyway, however reluctantly. As for the hotel, he wants to be sure to get the best room and the table on the veranda with the best view . . . It takes time to arrange all this . . ."

He listed, with great exaggeration, the weaknesses of Mario the parvenu. Mario was indeed a nouveau riche, but he was much more nouveau than riche and, to his regret, could hardly afford this kind of royal treatment.

But the important thing was to keep on talking, talking . . .

"For heaven's sake, what should I tell him?" Fulvia interrupted him again.

"Tell him to have a great time. Tell him to buy himself a suit of white Irish linen—make that six suits of white Irish linen . . ."

"Fabrizio, all he wants to know is when I plan to take my vacation. What should I tell him?"

"How should I know?"

Fulvia laid down her fork and put her hand on top of Fabrizio's.

The touch was warm and delicate, like that of a skilled, veteran jockey on the neck of a frightened horse.

"I just want to have some idea, in case we decide to go to Yugoslavia like last year, or somewhere else, some place where you want to go. What period do you think you'd prefer?"

Fabrizio's hand wriggled in hers like a fish caught in a net.

"But that's so many months away! Who knows what will happen to me, you and the rest of the world between now and this summer? We'll see, for God's sake!"

"Fine. But if we should happen to survive until then? If nuclear war doesn't break out? If our favorite places do not crumble to dust in some major cataclysm, when would you prefer to go—in July, August or September?"

Well, that's that, thought Fabrizio. A couple of smiles, a few bites to eat and she's already pulled out the straitjacket. That damned mania of hers for trapping him and forcing him to make decisions.

The little museum in Thebes had recently brought together a group of sarcophagi from the Mycenaean era unearthed by a German team and not yet catalogued or publicized. Fabrizio's sister, Teodora, had just happened to be there not long before and had succeeded in taking a pirate photo of one. The moment Fabrizio had seen it (the four birds in flight, modeled in polychrome terra-cotta at the corners of the urn, seemed about to carry the vessel up to the sky), he had decided to go to Thebes, with Fulvia of course . . . But it was one thing to indulge in solitary dreams in which she was a welcome presence—indeed, a desired, necessary presence—and it was something else entirely to bind oneself to a plan as though signing one's name on a promissory note . . .

"I don't know and I don't want to think about it," he shouted. To be called upon, in the month of April, to make commitments for July, August or September seemed to him an inhuman constraint that filled him with an intolerable feeling of claustrophobia. It was like taking the days between now and then and turning each one into a prison.

"I don't want to think about it," he repeated, trying to keep his voice from turning shrill and petulant, as it usually did when he became defensive or was trying to avoid a trap. "Do what you want, decide for yourself and don't make impossible demands of me."

Fulvia drew her hand away from Fabrizio's and put a meatball into her mouth, turning the innocent gaze of her hazel eyes on him.

"Nobody said we have to spend our vacation together," she said.

Right. So she would go around showing off her tits all by herself, fancy that. He was not too keen on this idea, not at all, but neither did he want to be forced to make promises. What in God's name did others do in these cases? Why did the simplest things always have to be so terribly difficult for him? He grabbed for the nearest excuse, just to buy some time.

"The fact is that I have to leave as soon as possible to look into something that I can't tell you about right now, something connected to work . . . If all goes well, we can take a very nice vacation together, almost as nice as the ones Mario treats himself to; and I'll finally have the honor of inviting you, the way civilized people do . . ."

"But it's fine with me if we go dutch. I only wanted to know when."

"Let me finish. The fact is that if this thing does not go well, I will have thrown away a lot of money for nothing and will have to spend the summer in Milan doing boring technical translations, the only kind that pay as they should."

"Have you stumbled across something big, a find?"

"I think so, but don't tell anyone."

Fulvia paused to reflect for a moment.

"I can lend you half a million lire. I imagine you're broke as usual." Just like that, with her customary unshakable kindness. She had understood his position, had accepted it and was immediately ready to help him. Fabrizio blushed, grew confused, refused her offer, went to look for his bankbook, did a few calculations together with Fulvia—still without telling her the purpose of his voyage—and finally accepted.

"This is all very unusual," he said, "and the fact that we're living in the last quarter of the twentieth century doesn't make me feel any less embarrassed."

"What nonsense."

"I'll pay you back."

"Let's hope so."

She wrote a check in her nice round handwriting and then slipped off her sweater as she headed toward the bedroom. She lifted up one foot, kicked off the shoe, stumbled a few steps down the corridor, then regained her balance and took off the other, vanishing behind the Russian literature bookcase, the outer limit of the so-called night zone.

Fabrizio joined her in the bedroom and found her busy pulling down the bedcovers. Her entire "look," so eagerly excessive—the tweed, raw silk and oiled leather, each article with its sacrosanct designer label—was either hanging, folded up or draped on a chair, leaving her firm limbs and golden skin wrapped in nakedness alone, serene and aware.

"You are the Queen of Sheba," said Fabrizio as he hurriedly undressed and slipped into bed. He followed her with his eyes as she closed the shutters halfway and drew the curtains. One of his erotic fantasies was to take her by surprise, block her path, force her against a wall, tear off her clothing and make her cry out in shame and humiliation: to violate not so much her body as her modesty . . . And he always snapped out of this fantasy with the same words: "With Fulvia, no less!"

His first attempt at seducing her had been a miserable failure. He had felt put in his place, like an impertinent child. She had accepted his invitation to come up to his apartment after the movies, for a glass of lemonade; but since she had never been one to read between the lines or to convey double messages herself, she came upstairs only to drink a glass of lemonade, nothing more. When he put his hands on her she merely gave him a peck on the cheek—gentle, curt, peremptory —and said: "That's enough"—calmly, without raising her voice. Just a few evenings later, after her own desire to make love had had a chance to ripen, she didn't need any coaxing; it all happened very smoothly and on cue, as though the two of them were Fred Astaire and Ginger Rogers in the most graceful of their dances.

With time, the more it became clear to Fabrizio that Fulvia was both physically and morally inviolable, the more his fantasies remained fixed on her, on that reserve of strength in her slim wrists and dauntless hazel eyes, her principles and decisiveness.

But that April afternoon—before Fulvia returned to relieve Mario of some of his duties—it was this same strength that discouraged Fabrizio from confiding in her, from seeking her help beyond the money for the trip. The feelings of inadequacy and mistrust of everyone, which had begun to ferment and seethe inside of him that morning had taken him light-years away from her resolute nature—she who never minced words, who distinguished so effortlessly between yes and no, always pronouncing both words in the clearest of voices—had carried him far, far away, to a dark world of undergrowth where she could not reach him and pull him to safety.

After the brief moment of sanity that Fulvia had provided by coming to his house with her bag of food, Fabrizio was once again overwhelmed by a sense of confusion and intrigue. He was convinced that since fate had always robbed him of everything, it was now his turn to rob fate, to appropriate Fritz Oberhofer for himself without telling anyone, not even Mario. Not with the understandable reserve of an explorer who wants to discover an unknown land before anyone else, but stealthily, like a thief, like someone committing a forbidden act. It was impossible to share such a state of mind with a person who was clarity incarnate. And so Fabrizio, as he lay next to Fulvia in the half-light after their lovemaking—an excellent moment for confidences—missed the chance, his last, to stay in touch with common sense, and set off alone toward his nightmare.

6

IT WAS TOO EXPENSIVE to fly to Vienna; the cost of the ticket alone would have used up almost half of the funds at his disposal, including what Fulvia had lent him. A travel agent had provided Fabrizio with all the information he needed to plan his voyage, and he now sat at his desk, studying the brochures and schedules. The Saint Jerome painted by a Flemish master four centuries earlier gazed out at him, engrossed. In that small, seventy-by-forty-centimeter frame, *he* had everything: books—all human knowledge packed into his little study bathed in golden light; the universe—the movements of the stars, the germinating power of seeds, the rhythm of the tides, outside the window but still within his grasp, and represented in all its vastness by the little goldfinch perched on the balcony; the consoling friendship of a loyal creature— the lion of the desert, curled up like a sleeping house cat. And in his heart, the gift of faith, the most formidable armor of all.

Something that Fabrizio felt had been shadowing him for the last fifteen years of his life was now taking hold of him, making his head spin, and it was the terrible sensation of having no protection: no money, no influential, well-disposed acquaintances, no well-defined and universally recognized entitlements. Like someone standing in the dark who prefers not to extend his arms so as not to feel the void surrounding him, he had managed, until now, to keep that sensation at bay, always taking very short steps and avoiding all risks—such as writing for himself instead of translating others, or responding in full to Fulvia's affections, or entering the fray of human relations. . . .

But now he had to take the plunge and find a way to get to Vienna.

He actually would have much preferred going by car to even flying. Fabrizio had traveled the world in his lifetime but had never become a traveler. When he and Teodora were children, their parents often used to take them along on their wanderings through Europe and beyond, along with the obligatory Fräulein and later Miss Hazelwood and Mademoiselle Adine. Then, when Teodora was sixteen years old and he was fourteen, their parents began to send them off on their own, she to one university town and he to another, where they would spend their vacations improving their knowledge of foreign languages. But everything was always prearranged for them by the family: room and board, transportation, reservations and so forth. They were always housed, fed and taught according to agreements in which they had taken no part.

Ever since he'd been left poor and alone (a situation that lasted only a few months for Teodora, as she had soon married a rich man), he had traveled very little, and only to familiar places: to the Maremma, where his sister had a country house, and to Yugoslavia, the old summer nightmare of Miss Hazelwood, who always got terribly seasick aboard the *Teodora* and once she was on dry land lived in terror of the local people, whom she called "those frightful Turks" because she had once seen the minaret of a mosque above the rooftops of Bosnia. He also went occasionally to the Dolomites, where Mitzi, the bartender at the Monte Pana, spoke to him in the familiar form and only recently had stopped remarking how he had grown. Austria, for some reason, had never been included in the Garrones' itineraries; now that he was about to set off alone and with little money in his pocket to that unfamiliar country, Fabrizio suddenly realized how much he hated feeling like an outsider, and how carefully he had always unconsciously avoided situations that might provoke such a feeling. Even in Milan, he never set foot in a store or restaurant that was not already long familiar to him.

The fact that the language was not a problem did not change anything. He simply did not like the idea of having to ask for directions, to speak to individuals who not only were total strangers but belonged to a country of seven million complete unknowns. Going up there in his Volkswagen would already have been an improvement. Enclosed inside its convex shell he would have felt less exposed—still disoriented perhaps, but better protected.

Unfortunately, this was impossible. What with the gasoline (Austria, Fabrizio thought glumly, must be the only country in the world where gasoline costs as much as in Italy), the highway tolls and—barring any accident—a stop along the way, it would cost him almost as much as flying. He had no choice but to make the best of the only affordable means of getting there: a night train with second-class couchette for less than fifty thousand lire.

He went out again to the travel agency to buy his train ticket. Then, back home, he called what the brochure said was the cheapest of the few guesthouses located in the center of Vienna and reserved a room for ten days. He called the office to invite Fulvia to dinner at his house; to Mario he said only that he was leaving for the Maremma the next day and would be away for two weeks.

————— 7 —————

THE BANK didn't have Austrian schillings.

"How can that be? I have a reservation on tonight's train and am expected at the hotel tomorrow."

"You should have put in a request for them a week in advance," replied the teller, not sharing Fabrizio's dismay.

It was clear from the start that everything would go wrong.

"Should I try another bank?"

"They'd just tell you the same thing."

For a good fifteen minutes Fabrizio sat there in the bank, sinking into the blackest despair, before the same teller fished him out with a distracted gesture.

"Buy dollars. You can go anywhere with dollars."

"But that will cost me much more."

"On the contrary. At the moment, the international monetary situation is such that if you change your lire into dollars and then, on arrival in Austria, your dollars into schillings, you'll actually make a little profit."

"Little bastard," Fabrizio thought to himself, "you could have told me right away."

"Thank you," he said out loud. "Thank you very much, you're very kind."

* * *

46

His train was supposed to leave at 8:10 P.M., stop at Mestre to hook up with a group of sleeping cars coming from Rome, and then continue to Vienna. This was what he had been told by the travel agent.

At the platform, however, the only sign for a train departing at 8:10 P.M. bore the words: MESTRE (MUNICH). Munich? Fabrizio felt himself breaking out in a cold sweat, convinced he had bought a ticket for a train that did not exist. The travel agent clearly had not listened closely to him. Fabrizio felt bitterly reconfirmed in an old conviction: that in order to get anyone's attention, in order to make oneself heard, in order to find one's way, an inheritance of some sort, of any sort, was necessary—in this case, either the money to pay for a first-class sleeper, or else a perfect knowledge of the procedures governing the lives of the poor. He remembered how when he tried, more than once, to take advantage of the public health services, he had found himself lost and confused in a throng of patients who seemed to know everything, all of them brandishing mysterious little pieces of paper obtained who-knows-where, each of which bore a number as proof of entitlement to services; those people blithely entered the labyrinth of corridors, knew all the doctors by name and were on very familiar terms with the nurses.

He never did get as far as the outpatient clinic, and now he was afraid he would never make it to Vienna.

He turned to a railway worker: "Excuse me, could you tell me where this train is going?"

The man indicated, with an annoyed nod of the head and an equally disdainful index finger, the plainly visible sign and said, "To Munich, by way of Mestre." He did not add "idiot" to his reply, but it was implicit in his gesture. Fabrizio thought of George Orwell, who with heroic political sincerity had wanted to go and live among the destitute in order to experience firsthand the realities of misery. He thought he should have done the same himself, if not out of a noble, virtuous impulse, then at least to get some practical training.

He felt horror at the thought that he was setting off on an adventure in which he would continually be forced to ask for help from rude, hurried strangers. It was a good thing he had come to the station early. He started walking down the platform alongside the train bearing the absurd sign MESTRE (MUNICH), until he reached the sleeping cars. The conductors of the Compagnie Internationale des Wagons-lit of his childhood had always seemed like paragons of politeness, second only to porters of fancy hotels. Things, of course, were different now: first of all, he himself was different, but most of all, he was no longer accompanied by his mother clad in sable, his authoritative stylish father, his sister, Teodora, and the Fräulein and their never-ending quarrels, along with the entire family's parade of pigskin suitcases. He didn't even have the minimal protection of a first-class ticket.

He ventured, nevertheless, to approach the conductor.

"I beg your pardon, but is this the train that hooks up, in Mestre, with the couchettes for Vienna?"

"This *should* be the train" was his sibylline reply.

"Oh my, what do you mean it *should* be?"

"Well, the couchettes come in from Rome, and sometimes, if they're late, we don't wait for them."

"Sometimes . . . ?"

"Yes, it all depends . . ."

At that moment it did not occur to Fabrizio how unlikely it was that a train full of Roman passengers unsuspectingly asleep in their couchettes and sure of waking up the next morning in Vienna could, on occasion, be left stranded on a dead-end track at the Mestre station.

He believed blindly what the conductor told him.

"But where does that leave me?" he cried out in despair. "I reserved a couchette . . . If you don't wait for the other train I'll have to ride all the way to Vienna sitting up."

The conductor looked up at him with eyes full of compassion.

"There's no guarantee that you'll get a seat if you haven't reserved one."

"What? A seat? But why in the world would I have reserved a seat when I had a couchette? Why? Can you please tell me?"

He felt like someone caught in the act, like an imbecile, a bungler who wanted to do things without following the rules but was miserably incapable of doing so. And that man had no intention of helping him; worse yet, he was hostile, he had something against him. In fact, he didn't answer Fabrizio's question, but continued, implacably:

"And there's especially no guarantee that you'll get to Vienna, even standing up."

That was it. He had known from the start that Vienna, for him, was an unreachable destination.

"And do you mind telling me why, for God's sake?"

"Because this train, with the exception of the engine, the sleeping car and one coach, is going to Munich."

Munich again. Railwaymen began closing doors and windows; the train would be leaving in a few minutes.

"Tell me, then," implored Fabrizio, "which is the coach that is definitely going to Vienna?"

"This one," he said, pointing to a car mobbed with people and marked, as far as Fabrizio could see, FIRST CLASS.

"Well, I guess I'll just have to stand in the corridor until we get to Mestre, and then if by some stroke of bad luck we don't hook up with the couchettes . . . How much is the difference that I would have to pay" ("Enough to ruin me," thought Fabrizio in his despair) "for a bed in your coach?"

"Oh, don't worry about that," replied the conductor, unconcerned. "In tourist class it's very inexpensive. It's just that . . ."

Oh, God. There was no end to the nightmare.

"Just what?"

"It's just that I have very few places left, and I don't know if they'll still be available by the time we get to Mestre."

So he would not be able to wait and see if the extra expense was necessary. He swallowed hard, straightened his back.

"Very well, I'll take a bed in tourist class."

It was less expensive than he had feared, only four times as much as the couchette he had already paid for, for which he surely would never receive a refund. He didn't know what he regretted most: the unexpected fleecing, the few thousand lire spent on the couchette he would never sleep in or the fact that he was unable to give the conductor the princely tip that he no doubt expected.

At Mestre, the cars from Rome were coupled up just as on any other night, but at that moment Fabrizio, knocked out by two sleeping pills, was already fast asleep in his bunk, squeezed in between an Italian student and a German tourist.

His first impression, upon arrival, was that either he did not know German, or this was not Vienna. The woman at the newsstand whom he had approached to ask which bus or tram would take him to Grabenstrasse, the street where his guesthouse was located, had answered him in an utterly incomprehensible idiom. He didn't even ask her to repeat what she had said, but merely headed, downcast, toward the line of people waiting for taxis. At this rate, he thought, he would use up all his money before ever setting foot inside the National Library. His very last resource seemed to have vanished with everything else: here he was in Vienna, the polyglot, former pupil of numerous German governesses and student of summer courses in Heidelberg and Frankfurt, and he didn't understand a single word of what anyone said to him.

The guttural sounds that the newspaperwoman had emitted seemed to conceal an obscure threat. They led one to imagine that there were secret requirements to be met, initiation rites to be performed before one could reach any desired goal whatsoever; that a man had to belong to a particular secret order, have his name on some unknown register . . .

He waited in line forever, while buses and trams sped by all around him. The queue of people waiting with him was not as orderly as he would have expected; indeed, the surprise attack seemed to be a more effective and more accepted method of getting a cab than calmly waiting one's turn. Perhaps, thought Fabrizio as he noticed the Mediterranean features of his companions-in-waiting, this was owing to the fact that the queue was not in the least composed of disciplined Viennese citizens. The Viennese, lucky stiffs, could take the tram.

He realized that he would never get anywhere this way and so decided to try again to find out about public transportation. He went up and asked a man passing by with a cardboard box full of chirruping chicks. The man's reply was exactly the same as the newspaper vendor's, but he made more of an effort to be understood, using plenty of facial expressions and gesticulations.

This time Fabrizio understood, and on his way to the nearest stop of the D-line tram, he managed, by straightening out the dialect's twisted vowels in his mind, to reconstruct the words of the vendor and the man with the chicks. He had always talked with his governesses and his professors at Heidelberg and Frankfurt; but those were privileged encounters, made possible by wealth. Would his last inheritance, his linguistic skill, prove useful in less fortunate circumstances?

As the tram passed along the walls of the Belvedere Gardens, Fabrizio felt certain it would. He had found a seat. The driver was a woman, a handsome blonde who before each stop announced the name of the station and the connecting lines in a smooth, perfectly accented voice.

Sumptuous and stately, Prince Eugene's palace appeared bit by bit to Fabrizio's right, through the gates that afforded a glimpse within the surrounding wall. In a few hours' time he would learn to understand the Viennese dialect. The tram driver was charming, and Fabrizio began to feel welcome in the city.

—————— 8 ——————

AT THE NATIONAL LIBRARY he found four novels by Fritz Oberhofer, but *Das Haus am Mondsee* was not one of them.

"Excuse me, Fräulein, but I know there's a fifth book by the same author. You must have it."

Through thick glasses the librarian cast a cold blue stare at him.

"Here we have a copy of everything that has been published within the confines of the empire, sir. You must be mistaken. If you know of the existence of another work by this Fritz Oberhofer, it must be an unpublished manuscript."

She was very stern and sure of herself. She had the most efficient administration in modern history backing her up. He, however, came from a country where cultural and artistic treasures were often lost, left unprotected against thieves or forgotten in dark, damp cellars. This was yet another point of vulnerability that he hadn't considered. Who indeed was he to tell this woman what was or was not in the National Library of Vienna?

"I guess it is possible that it's not here . . . I mean, I'm sure it's not here, if you say it's not . . . but, you see, I know that in 1913 someone read it, and, as with the other four, that only one hundred copies were printed, for private circulation . . . Therefore, I beg you—it's not here, agreed—but please don't tell me it doesn't exist. . . ."

All his hopes hung on the librarian's verdict; she seemed to have the power not only to impart the truth but to determine it as well; to determine, today, with a single word, whether or not Fritz Oberhofer published, in 1913, *Das Haus am Mondsee*. Pasquali's authority dissolved into nothingness next to hers.

Perhaps it was Fabrizio's face—with all his hopes slipping down the drain, he didn't try to control himself, maintain his dignity or hide his childlike look of desperation, so touching to behold in its naked intensity; whatever it was, the librarian finally took pity on him.

"A hundred copies printed for private circulation?"

"Yes."

"At the author's expense?"

This was something Fabrizio did not know for certain, since Pasquali made no mention of it, but it seemed like a point that might make the librarian more favorably disposed toward negotiation.

"Yes, of course; at the author's expense."

"Nothing of importance, in other words . . ."

"Good heavens, I'm well aware that this Oberhofer was not at all well known . . ."

He had said "this Oberhofer" with just the right tone, he thought. It reduced the writer to a level of utter insignificance, making him a nothing, a nobody, so that it became justifiable, almost proper and fitting, to have lost one of his novels.

"He wrote for pleasure," he went on. "He was probably rich, I imagine . . . and so, you know . . . just a few copies . . . for friends . . . and the delight of seeing one's work in print . . ."

"Of course, in certain circumstances, oversights do sometimes occur, even here . . . Less often than elsewhere, mind you: around here we have a certain talent for organization."

The look she gave Fabrizio left no doubt in his mind that she had been to Italy before, perhaps to the National Library in Rome, or on platform 15 at the central station in Milan, to catch the 8:10 P.M. train for Vienna . . .

"Yes, of course, who could deny it."

"And then the Great War broke out shortly thereafter . . . There was a bit of confusion, no doubt . . . *Es tut mir Leid*, I'm sorry, sir. The book you are looking for is not here; but there's a chance it *might*, I say *might*, have been printed, if you have good reason to believe so."

This was all the help the librarian could give him. Fabrizio stayed in the library until closing time to read the other four books; they were all skimpy little volumes entirely devoid of value, conventional, boring and false.

He did not let the four inferior novels discourage him. On the contrary, he took comfort in the fact that they provided a logical explanation for the indifference with which *Das Haus am Mondsee* had been received; it was quite understandable that no one would have bothered to read it when his other works had proven to be of so little worth. And he was thrilled at the prospect that he, Fabrizio Garrone—whom fate had always taken delight in cheating, without ever bothering to compensate—would be the one to revive Fritz Oberhofer, to do him justice and win him the glory he deserved.

Oberhofer was a Germanic name, hence it was pointless to consult the archives of the synagogue or the Juden Rathaus.

The little relevant information that there was at the general registry office was uncovered in an instant, attesting to the bureaucratic excellence that had inspired such pride in the librarian. Siegfried Oberhofer had moved to Vienna from Innsbruck in 1830. With the help of his wife, Esther, he set up a small factory for making men's and women's hats. Siegfried and Esther had three children, two boys and one girl; the first died at age twenty in a hunting accident; the second,

Anton, joined the family business at a very young age, bringing bold new ideas with him that eventually transformed the small operation into a flourishing industry.

He did not marry until he was forty. He lived at home with the family, cared for by his mother and later by his sister, who never married. His marriage did not last long, just long enough to provide him with an heir—little Friedrich—after which his frail wife expired, leaving everything just as it had been before, or so one might imagine: the same house, the same habits, the same uncontested rule of Lieselotte, his spinster sister.

Fritz's great love was literature, not hats. In his will Anton generously bequeathed most of his fortune to a hospital, setting aside for his son a sum that would provide him with a life annuity enabling him to live in ease and comfort. The will also contained a clause stipulating that a part of the sum earmarked for the hospital would not come definitively into that institution's possession before Fritz's fiftieth birthday, and that if Fritz had any children before then, that portion of the inheritance would be returned to him.

The hospital still existed, and on one of its walls hung a commemorative plaque in honor of Anton Oberhofer, its benefactor; as for Fritz, nobody knew anything about him, aside from the fact that he never came forward before his fiftieth birthday to claim his due.

In fact, as the records at the registry office showed, Fritz Oberhofer died in 1913 at the age of thirty-eight, unmarried and childless. The eventual fate of his personal possessions— books, clothes, furniture—was anybody's guess.

In junk shops and secondhand book stores, Fabrizio managed to find only the first four novels, which he promptly bought. He returned to the library several times to look for information on Fritz Oberhofer that might provide some clue as to where he could find a copy of *Das Haus am Mondsee*.

He checked all the extant correspondence, biographies and memoirs of personalities of the Viennese cultural scene of the

as I am given to believe. Let us say good-bye to a friend who lived well on this earth and never needed to seek further reward in immortality."

Not a word about his last novel. Perhaps the printer had delivered the package with the hundred copies when Fritz was already seriously ill and unable to write the twenty or thirty letters he had probably wanted to send his friends along with copies of *Das Haus am Mondsee*. Fabrizio knew what those unwritten letters would have said, as well as if he had conceived them himself, lying in pain on a bed in shadow (I'll sit down to write them as soon as I feel a little better) . . . "Dear friend . . . I think I've finally succeeded this time . . . Forget my previous attempts and, as a token of your affection for me, please bear with me just once more . . ."

Or maybe the printer's package was never even delivered . . . The messenger rings the doorbell of the empty house. No answer. The woman next door pokes her head out of a window. "I'm sorry, but the man you're looking for died last week. There's nobody there anymore."

It might have happened that way, or some other way as well. What was certain was that one hunderd copies of the book had been printed, that one of these had fallen into Giorgio Pasquali's hands and that Fabrizio had every intention of finding one of the remaining ninety-nine.

Fate, which had been so good to Fritz Oberhofer, could hardly fail to keep this last promise. This no doubt was why it had set in motion a process which had reached its final stage almost seventy years later, entrusting the last act of reparation to Fabrizio Garrone. For the plan to be respected, absolute secrecy had to be maintained: Fabrizio's need to operate covertly had by now so outgrown its original, logical justification that it eclipsed all memory of it and marked his every word and action like some superstitious rite. His fear of being beaten to the task had swelled into an undefined terror, a primordial dread. To no one had he pronounced out loud the title of the novel he was looking for. At the library he had merely asked for "a fifth novel by Fritz Oberhofer"; the book-sellers and junk dealers let him poke about on his own without asking any questions.

By now he had compiled a rich, detailed file. Looking it over, he concluded that after 1910 Fritz lost touch with all of his friends, to the point that none of them had any idea he had written another novel in the last three years of his life. Fabrizio almost felt glad that it was pointless to go knocking at the doors of their descendants: he would have had to give explanations, pronounce the secret name. He preferred to wander about at random, hoping that luck would eventually lead him to a copy of *Das Haus am Mondsee*.

He asked to keep his room at the guesthouse for another week, but no sooner had he done this than seven days seemed like a very long time, a waste of money, an eternity of loneliness. He missed Fulvia, although he could not remember a single moment with her, especially of late, that he had not managed to spoil with his inability to give himself over freely to love.

He decided, since he was already there, to visit the city like any other tourist, to give some sort of justification to his chaotic quest.

$$9$$

HE GOT OFF THE TRAM at the gates to the Belvedere Gardens. It was nine in the morning and the sun shone hot on leaves still moist from the night before, producing waves of fragrance that penetrated deep into Fabrizio's psyche and awakened an old memory, like a ray of light in a dark room.

The hedges of the Italian garden that sloped down toward the orderly city beyond Prince Eugene's palace were neither yews nor myrtles, as one might have expected, but thujas, arborvitae, well pruned and compressed into geometric shapes.

There used to be a large thuja in front of the house in Genoa; people who saw it said it was the biggest they'd ever seen. One clear June morning twenty years earlier, that tree began to give off a fragrance it seemed to have been storing up for years, as though it wanted everyone to set a bit of that sweetness aside and remember it forever. Fabrizio remembered. That morning his mother died, her Henri de Montherlant novel fallen facedown into the grass. He remembered the wicker chaise longue, the singing finches, the butterflies in the air, the honeysuckle's winding branches, the silk shirtwaist the color of wisteria that his mother was wearing that day, the tailored outfits and cashmere sweaters she wore in winter, the whole succession of garments that went back, with slight, almost unnoticeable alterations from one link in the chain to the next, to the wardrobes of her grandmother, her great-grandmother, her great-great-grandmother. His mother had not been especially intelligent, witty or even generous; but she had style. And her style, like that thuja so large that it took four people to embrace it, was ancient, rooted, natural. Teodora, who was bright, cheerful, free-spirited, and on the surface seemed not to resemble any of the women in the family, was deep down just like the rest of them, and the chain remained unbroken.

But what had this heritage passed down to him, aside from a cursed sense of awkwardness, of ineptitude at living, of never fitting in? Assailed from all sides by the mournful, age-old fragrance of thuja, he saw the shadow of his body cast in the morning sun as a blot too dark, too opaque, an unseemly presence—both there in the Belvedere Gardens and, going back in his mind to the last few days, at Schönbrunn and in the courtyards of the Hofburg, where everything was not merely well preserved but kept ready, as it were, as though the rightful owners might at any moment decide to rise up from the Capuchin crypt and reclaim possession of their former dwellings.

Amid the vestiges of that empire lost and then restored by time, once and for all, to the dead, Fabrizio felt his entire consciousness gripped by the certainty that he was the only person on earth with nothing he could lay claim to as his own, clearly and with authority, the way Adelmo Basso, Fulvia's father, had reclaimed payment from a delinquent client.

He decided to forget about visiting the city's monuments and wandered absentmindedly through the streets, no longer knowing where to look next.

The lost novel was always on his mind. His loneliness took him to the old cafés and beer halls that Fritz had probably frequented. He would sit there, imagining himself as the writer, staring at the empty seat in front of him, seeking the company of ghosts. He did not try to reconstruct in his mind the words, gestures and tender looks that make up a happy love affair. All he knew from experience was that as soon as a chance encounter between two strangers took on the weight and form of a love bond, it began to sour.

Unless it was the other way around, and he was confusing cause and effect. Perhaps the boredom, the resentment and the subtle, mutual hostility were not so much the consequence of a deepening of ties as a mechanism that set off in him the desire to deepen them. Indeed, no sooner would a woman become insufferable to him than he would begin to see her fairly regularly. Usually only five, ten times, of course the longest of his ill-fated adventures in sentiment having lasted a month in all.

Except for Fulvia. With her, things could have been altogether different, and he was well aware of this. And yet even with her, he still carried around inside himself that old, perverse vice of his.

Fritz, on the other hand, had known the joys of a life spent traveling the sweet paths of happiness and tenderness; Fabrizio followed him around with eyes closed, not bothering to keep track of where he was going. He sat at the tables of cafés and beer halls, in the company of ghosts; he listened to their voices as though they were the sounds of birds singing, a melodious and incomprehensible language.

He loved Karin most of all. She had been tempted away from him by another, and this made her even more beautiful, more precious. But she had remained true to him, had surrendered her coveted woman's heart only to him. This filled him with the humblest adoration and, at the same time, made him proud to be so honored.

Fabrizio found a 1915 photograph of her sitting at the piano, no longer so fresh and youthful. She was living in America and had achieved a certain amount of success. Fritz was already two years dead. She had kept her slender figure, and the gray hair on her high forehead looked like a queen's tiara. She probably had sweet memories of Vienna. When he imagined her sitting before him, he saw her as both girl and woman, innocent and severe, tender and impetuous.

Entranced by the sweetness of the unfathomable loves of others, Fabrizio realized he was wasting time. It was true his room did not cost very much, but it was sheer madness to stay in Vienna after having combed every last corner where the disregarded, forgotten masterpiece might be hidden. He had stopped looking yet stayed on, each day postponing his return to Italy, waiting for something, though he knew not what.

One morning he woke up less weary and bewildered than usual. It had rained all night, and now the sun glistened on the rooftops and the buds of the linden trees. He decided to play one last card and put a classified ad in the *Courier*.

There was no way in the world he was going to name *Das Haus am Mondsee*. He wrote: "I am looking for novels by Fritz Oberhofer." But later, just as he was about to turn in his ad to the "classifieds" window, it occurred to him that even this wording violated the code of occult laws to which he felt so deeply bound. He rationalized to himself that an advertisement worded this way ran the risk of arousing an unwelcome curiosity about the forgotten writer; he had to ask for other things as well, thereby camouflaging Fritz Oberhofer's novels amid an intricate hodgepodge of other requests.

Try as he might, he could think of nothing that might serve this purpose, and so he went around to the junk shops in the old city and ended up buying four knickknacks from the period immediately preceding the First World War: a calendar, a military cap, a playbill and an issue of the *Osterreichische Rundschau*. He then rewrote his ad, mixing the books in with the other odds and ends, and turned it in to the newspaper at once, not allowing himself any time for second thoughts.

He had given the address and telephone number of the hotel

for anyone who might want to reach him, and for two whole days he stayed in his room, waiting for callers. On the little table in his room he lined up the four objects he had bought in junk shops, seeing this as the only way to turn down any hustler who might try to sell him the same things. It was his way of keeping things under control. He even had his answer ready: "As you can see, I've already found it, but thank you just the same."

One strange character after another showed up, seedy types, all bearing among their wares either the kepi, the playbill or the magazine; several of them had the calendar. None, however, brought books, not even the ones Fabrizio had already bought.

Finally someone called from Graz, offering to send him, C.O.D., *Die Zauberin*.

"Thank you, but I've already found it," he said, picking the book up from his bedside table and holding it next to the receiver. It was the truth; everything was working out according to plan; he could relax.

On the second day, at about ten in the evening, the last hopeful peddler arrived.

He was carrying a brown paper package, which he set down on the bed.

"You're interested in Viennese life before the Great War, if I'm not mistaken? . . . A historian, I suppose? . . . Or perhaps just . . . a dilettante?"

He pronounced the last word in an insinuating manner, leaning against the package, which was slowly coming undone, and casting a long sidelong glance at Fabrizio.

"Many things have disappeared," he continued, his voice now a whisper, "but others still remain . . . You just have to know who to turn to, that's all."

By now the string around the package had come untied, and the flaps that had kept the paper folded down over itself had opened up, so that one merely had to pull the two ends apart to get at the contents.

"Who knows? Perhaps you were looking for . . . this?"

In the middle of the open packet was a braid of black hair.

"Good Lord, no," stammered Fabrizio. "Absolutely not."

What did this joker want? In his ad he had asked for nothing of the sort. The fellow probably had something devious, sinister, up his sleeve.

The man stood up again and eyed him mischievously. He was tall, brawny and looked about sixty. He was clad in traditional Tyrolean dress, gray cloth jacket with little green insignias, tight-fitting lederhosen that went down to just below the knee and silver buttons. Upon entering he had laid his little green hat, with its tuft of feathers tucked inside the ribbon, on the chair. He had short grey hair, cut especially short at the back of his neck. His face was fat, pink and smooth, his features indistinct, his eyes seeming to float on the surface of his skin. It was as though his creator had remained uncertain for a long time as to what sort of physiognomy to give him and in the end decided not to give him any. He was as Austrian as a mannikin in one of the large department stores on the Mariahilferstrasse, and every bit as indistinguishable a specimen as any of them.

"My advertisement," said Fabrizio, "made no mention of anything . . . like that."

The man waved his hand in a gesture of disregard.

"What's the difference? What's the difference if it's one thing instead of another? I have brought you, as you can read on the label"—and he picked up the braid and brought it close to Fabrizio's face, making him jump back in horror— "I have brought you a braid of hair worn by the great Olga Lederer for the world premiere of Richard Strauss's *Salome* in 1912, here in Vienna."

The man was a swindler and made no attempt to hide it. The premiere of *Salome* had not taken place in Vienna, nor in

1912, and there had never been a great soprano, or any other singer, named Olga Lederer.

"You see," continued the Tyrolean mannikin, "when she played Salome she would pin the braid to the top of her head, as the label tells you, and then let it fall right before performing the dance of the seven veils. The hair, as you can imagine, would dance along with her like a nest of serpents. Watch . . ."

He loosed the braid and shook it about, making his way around the bed in soft little steps, half-turns and short bows. The black tresses writhed and twisted wildly.

"As you can see, I can find anything, anything you want."

From his pocket he drew out a comb with very few teeth and began to stroke Salome's tresses.

"Think about it . . . Would you mind holding this for a moment?"

Fabrizio, in disgust, found himself holding the long black tail at the end where the strands were attached to a tortoiseshell clasp. With great dexterity the man rebraided it, wrapped it in the paper and tied up the bundle.

"Think about it," he repeated. "I can find you anything, as long as you tell me what it is you really want."

"My good man, my advertisement is quite explicit . . . and as you can see for yourself," he said, gesturing toward the objects lined up on the table, "I've already found everything I need."

The man pulled a newspaper clipping out of his jacket pocket.

"It seems to me you're still missing something," he said. "Ah, yes. Books."

Could this man possibly be the one who would find him *Das Haus am Mondsee?* He seemed so dubious, so shady . . . Fabrizio had been a fool to have the newspaper print an advertisement composed in that manner. Any shrewd person, such as this fellow was, would have realized that all those objects, except one, were listed to hide the one important

66

thing, to draw attention away from it. The man had clearly understood that there was a treasure hunt behind all this, and now he was planning to blackmail Fabrizio by threatening to call attention to him.

Only for a brief moment did Fabrizio stop to think that he might be exaggerating, that the feeling of strangeness to which he had abandoned himself might be carrying him too far, making him see plots, shady characters and mysterious coincidences at every turn; but that sudden flash of common sense was too short-lived, and his fears immediately regained the upper hand.

"I've found those too," he hastened to assure the man. He took the novels of Fritz Oberhofer from the night table and shoved them under the Tyrolean's nose just as the other had done to him with the braid. "Still, that memento you showed me is rather interesting."

Would buying that foul thing help him to get rid of this crook . . . or would it merely prove he had something to hide, opening the door to more serious harassment?

Was that inscrutable mannikin just a cheap con man out for a quick swindle or was he aiming higher? As soon as Fabrizio had uttered his statement he regretted it.

The Tyrolean bowed ceremoniously.

"A very interesting memento indeed."

"How much do you want for it?"

"Two thousand schillings."

"That's too much. I'm a foreigner, a tourist. My funds are limited."

"A foreigner, of course. I could tell you were Italian from the elegance of your clothes . . . but certainly not from your accent, which, I must say, is quite flawless. My compliments. Eighteen hundred."

"Seventeen."

They agreed on a price of one thousand seven hundred and fifty schillings. Fabrizio walked the man to the door and then locked it behind him. He tossed the bundle with the braid, as well as all the objects lined up on the table, into the wastepaper basket and went to sleep.

At dawn he was awakened by an anxiety that had worked its way into his sleep. What if someone . . . it was ridiculous, but what if someone had been watching him, someone who knew about his advertisement and found out that none of that stuff was of any interest to him whatsoever? Furtive as a spy in a movie, he retrieved all the objects and put them and the Fritz Oberhofer novels into a plastic bag, which he placed at the back of the closet.

10

THE FOLLOWING DAY, as he wandered about the city, Fabrizio thought he saw the man in Tyrolean dress. For a brief moment he was almost certain he had recognized him, but the little green hat quickly disappeared in the crowd.

He had to find the book and get out of Vienna.

He went into a café and ordered a piece of Käsetorte. As he nibbled idly at the cake, he tried to imagine the plot of that elusive novel. A house on the lake—probably a small lake in the Alps that reflected the moon; a legend surrounding the lake; real characters whose life stories were interwoven with the age-old fables of the region. A novel of the night, suspended between myth and reality. . . .

A man in Tyrolean dress had entered the café. Fabrizio could see him only from behind. The stranger headed toward the far end of the room, still with his back to him, and stopped at a corner table near the door to the rest rooms. He sat down, turning toward Fabrizio, but remained in the shadows, so that his face was only a circle of white.

He had to get out of Vienna.

And give up?

In any case, he had to get out of that café at once; then he would give it some thought.

While the desk clerk at the guesthouse was looking for his key, Fabrizio, not wanting to lose sight of the door behind him, raised his eyes toward the large mirror in front of him. Attached to one corner of the glass was a travel poster. The large color photograph showed a number of young people fishing while others were preparing a barbecue on a very green lawn.

Below the photo were the words *Sommerferien am Mondsee*, summer vacation on the Mondsee. There it was. So Moon Lake was not a setting invented by Fritz Oberhofer; it really existed. Why had he not thought of this earlier? Perhaps because it was such a pretty name it had never occurred to him that it might be real. But it was every bit as real as Lake Como, Lake Tahoe, Lake Titicaca. With his heart in his mouth, he dashed up the stairs, too excited to wait for the hotel's decrepit elevator. His hair danced across his forehead, his eyes sparkled. His arms and legs obeyed him famously.

He took the map of Austria out of his suitcase. With the door locked behind him, he looked for the Mondsee. He found it immediately. It was S-shaped, quite small and near Salzburg.

At the Salzburg train station he tossed the black braid, the issue of *Österreichische Rundschau*, the playbill and the calendar into a waste can. He tucked the four Fritz Oberhofer novels into a corner of his suitcase and put the soldier's cap on his head. He knew the way as well as if he were going to his own house. He was singing *"Fin ch'han dal vino"* at the top of his lungs as he crossed the station square looking for the bus that would take him to Mondsee.

It was a local bus, which did not go by way of the Autobahn but took the old national road instead, stopping at every small cluster of houses.

Fabrizio still felt cheerful and still had the kepi on his head,

70

though he had stopped singing. He remembered an old cliché often used to describe the houses, clothes and gardens of those eccentric personalities to whom we ascribe brilliant, irreverent ideas, delightfully odd habits, hearts of gold and madness bordering on genius; the expression was "picturesque disorder," and it had entered his thoughts because the surrounding countryside with its woods, meadows and hamlets was, like a flower about to bloom, bursting with picturesque order.

The trees that covered the hills in dense harmony came to an end at the edge of a meadow, the last branches bent down low enough to touch the grass with just-budded leaves. Crystal-clear streams were flanked by bright green fields, clusters of willows and here and there a slender crescent of white sand. Every house had its little stack of firewood resting in a sheltered spot near the kitchen door, and every stack was a neat, well-ordered parallelepiped whose perfect balance no single log dared upset by jutting out or tilting.

Each house was surrounded by a small yard filled with flowers and fruit trees, and around each yard was a well-painted fence; then, between the road and the house was a strip of grass of even width, bordered by a bicycle path, bordered by an identical strip of grass. There was not an inch of *terrain vague*, not a single discarded object. Here and there, one could see small structures at various stages of building, but nothing showed signs of chronic incompletion or progressive decay.

Hardly any passengers boarded the bus when it stopped, but many got off, and soon Fabrizio found himself alone with the driver. He went and sat near to him.

"Do you think I'll be able to find a room at a guesthouse in Mondsee?" he asked the driver.

"Sure. Many of them stay open year round. Where would you like to go?"

"Oh, anywhere, as long as it's not expensive."

"In town or on the lake?"

"On the lake would be wonderful."

"I know where to take you. Normally there's no stop there, but I'm running early today and there won't be any more passengers getting on before the end of the line . . . Over there, you see? Get off here, that way you save yourself a half-kilometer walk. Have a good stay!"

The guesthouse, built of white masonry and dark wood, stood on a small strip of grass. It was shielded from behind by the woods and gave directly onto the lake.

There were two or three people in the dining room drinking beer, obviously locals. The rooms at that time of year were all vacant and Fabrizio could have the best in the house. "*Aber freilich*"—but of course, the landlady had said when asked, the one with a view of the lake.

Fabrizio noticed that the woman had the same friendly smile as the bus driver and the peaceful countryside he had crossed to get there. Ever since he had first set eyes on the travel poster in the Vienna hotel, everything seemed to be telling him that luck for once was on his side. Now the final confirmation of this hope lay right before his eyes, for in the glass show-case behind the hotel desk was a book.

It stood there together with a large stuffed fish with a sinister look on its face, a signed photograph of Franz Lehar, a silver cup won by a certain Joseph Wünsch at a horse show held in Sterzing in 1906 and an old-fashioned deer-hunting rifle. It was displayed like a painting, propped flat against the back of the showcase so that all could plainly see the yellow cover with the title printed diagonally across it in florid lavender Gothic lettering: Fritz Oberhofer—*Das Haus am Mondsee*.

Fabrizio signed the register that the woman held out to him.

"That's quite a fish," he observed, not letting his voice quaver from the excitement he felt. "Can one still catch monsters like that around here?"

He passed himself off as an avid fisherman. The landlady had nothing to do for the moment. This young Italian was good-looking, with those intense, expressive green eyes set against their black lashes. Very *temperamentvoll*. She leaned against the desk with her huge round breasts, which were covered by her muslin blouse but accentuated by the pink corselet of her traditional dress, and got ready for a nice long chat.

Fabrizio asked her about fishing licenses for tourists, inquired into the price of a room for the period from June 10 to June 30. He talked about bait, currents, boats.

"And that book," he finally said offhandedly. "Is it about the fishing on this lake?"

"I wouldn't know," replied the landlady. "I've so little time for reading. It's always been there, for as long as I can remember."

"Do you think I could borrow it? I'd love to read it."

He'd done it. He read until dawn: it was a beautiful novel.

First thing in the morning he went out with the book hidden under his raincoat and into town to have it photocopied. Then he returned to his room and locked the copies in his suitcase.

"It's only a novel," he said to the landlady as he handed the book back to her. "Too bad. It doesn't say anything about fishing."

He set off for Milan and arrived home late that night.

The next morning he called Fulvia at the office.

"I found it," he said. "It seemed impossible—nowhere else to turn, a disaster. Then, by a stroke of luck, I found it."

"You found what?"

"But of course, you don't know anything about it . . ." How could he ever have gone off without confiding to Fulvia his secret plans and hopes, especially after having accepted the money she had so generously offered to lend him? What sort of petty, vulgar, loathsome boor was he to have acted so mysteriously with a woman like Fulvia?

"Can you talk?" he whispered.

"What?"

"Is Mario there?"

"No, he's at the printer's. What's with you anyway?"

"It all began three weeks ago, the day you came to have lunch and then wrote me that check. Well, that morning I found a book at an old kiosk . . ."

Unable to control his excitement, he told her everything, his words pouring out in waves.

"Then finally," he said, "there it was in the showcase, in the middle of all those worthless knicknacks."

Fabrizio felt a lump rising in his throat as he continued talking: "It's a masterpiece, Fulvia. Fritz Oberhofer is a great writer, God bless him. I wish he would come back to life so I could hug him; I want to go pray at his grave, to honor him in every way possible, as he deserves."

"You will, you will. You'll bring him the fame he never knew. *You* will be the one to do it, after sixty years when no one even knew he had ever lived. But why don't you want to tell Mario about it?" She fell silent for a moment, then in a lowered voice said: "You don't want to have it published by someone else, do you? You wouldn't do a thing like that . . . would you?"

"It never even crossed my mind. I just want to do it alone, without interference. I want to be able to bring it to him when it's ready."

This wasn't really true, but since Fabrizio himself didn't know what the truth was, he made do with this explanation.

"I'm going to start translating at once. I don't even want to think about anything until I've finished."

"Good, that's what I like to hear. And don't worry about dinner tonight; I'll bring it over. Work well."

She showed up at seven-thirty, weighed down by two plastic shopping bags and a suitcase, her leather moccasins sticking to the floor like suction cups, common sense and reason shining in the golden light of her hair and packed, without an inch of wasted space, in that fearless, energetic little body of hers.

Her little Lombard face was vibrant with adoration and

74

goodwill, like the face of a puppy presenting its first mole to its venerated master.

"I'll stay here with you until you've finished," she announced. "I'll do your shopping, cook your meals, keep things in order, so you can work in peace."

She made room for her things in the closet and began to hang up her clothes as she took them out of the suitcase. For once, Fabrizio did not compare them with his mother's Lanvins or his sister's extravagant rags.

"My dear little angel," he said, "so, so sweet." He held her tightly to him, kissing her soft, downy hair. "You're an angel, a warrior angel, generous and brave . . . A fair knight *sans peur et sans reproche*."

"I'm protecting my investment," said Fulvia, smiling.

Mario lost all contact with Fabrizio; or rather, he failed to reestablish contact with him, even though he knew he was back from his trip. He had known almost from the start that Fabrizio did not go to the Maremma, because he had run into Teodora by chance.

"He's gone away," Fulvia had told him. "Where, I don't know. It's for some job." And in fact, at the time this was all she knew.

But even later, after Fabrizio had confided in her, she kept his secret.

"He's working and doesn't want any help, advice or interference. He knows what he's doing. Let him be. He'll come to you when he's done."

Mario complied and was very discreet. Every evening he would see Fulvia come back from doing the shopping and then disappear with her plastic bags into Fabrizio's apartment building. In the morning he would see her come out again. His usual jealousy, which he had always kept well under control, had changed form and object. He was both jealous and curious —but now these emotions were focused on Fabrizio rather than on her. He felt almost torn in half: it was the first time that Fabrizio had dispensed with his care, thus depriving him of the double outlook on the world that he had grown accustomed to having.

He had been ordered not to interfere, and he did as he was told.

11

FULVIA SAW to all of Fabrizio's needs; he worked feverishly, exaltedly. Fritz Oberhofer came back to life with each new sentence, preparing to receive the glory that was his due. The German flowed smoothly and naturally, settling into a melodious, parallel Italian. The transformation came about without effort.

"It falls into place all by itself," Fabrizio said to Fulvia one evening at dinner. "It slides around, flips over, then finds its own way, like a dolphin in water. It's as though Fritz wrote just to be translated by me, and I learned German just to translate him."

"You shouldn't talk that way. I don't like it, you sound . . . I don't know, like someone obsessed. It's a beautiful book, and you know your craft very well. It's as simple as that."

"You don't understand . . . it's more than that. There's a kind of affinity . . . it's hard to explain. As I progress with the translation, it's as though there exists, inside me, a free, fluid vision not yet flattened into words. It's what comes *before*—the ghost before it has assumed form in one language or another . . . I know how I must translate because I am already familiar with these formless images; I have them inside me . . . It's true, you have to believe me, it's just as I say."

Fulvia was not one to indulge in gratuitous meditation. She made good use of her intelligence, but only in the service of concrete goals. She realized that Fritz Oberhofer could give Fabrizio the chance to step out of his present role, a rather limited one for a person of his talent, which she judged to be immense. But she also believed that the relationship between the dead author and the living translator should be limited, as though by a contract with a due date, the sole purpose of which would be to grant the former the fame denied him when alive while establishing the latter as the brilliant man of letters that he was. But that was all, and when it was over, it was time to move on to something else. Fabrizio's infatuation or, worse yet, his ridiculous identification with Fritz conjured up in her mind visions of a desolate, barren future for him, an eternity of turning round and round in circles, content to scrape about in ever more obscure corners, asking ever more irrelevant questions, falling inexorably into the role of the fool, the madman.

She got up from her place and approached Fabrizio, who was still sitting at the table. She pressed him to her breast, stroking his hair.

"You shouldn't talk like that. It's only because you're good, the best of them all. I know that my opinion doesn't count for much, but someone who knows about these things once told me . . . 'Your Fabrizio,' he said, 'has a feeling for the language.' "

"Who told you that?"

"Guido Ribelli. He has just now published a study on Hölderlin—"

"I know who he is. How long have you known him?"

"A while."

"And I imagine you've also been to bed with him, and recently at that, if he refers to me as 'your Fabrizio.' "

"It was last year, if you really want to know. Last year,

when for at least two months you didn't say a single thing to me that wasn't obnoxious. I don't like to be alone. And when you treat me that way, I don't see why I should."

How could anyone deny the truth of words so plain? Fabrizio brimmed with tenderness. Sheltered and protected in Fulvia's bosom, he wrapped his arms around her small waist, and let her cradle him like a child.

"You won't be alone anymore. Everything's going to change when I'm finished."

"Because of Fritz Oberhofer?"

"Among other things."

Fabrizio finished the translation in a month. The introduction, however, cost him a great deal of effort. He wrote and rewrote it, and not until the fourth draft did he feel satisfied, if not overly enthusiastic.

That morning he got up at five. Fulvia joined him a little bit later, still half-asleep, bringing him a coffee from the kitchen.

"How's it going?"

"I'm almost done."

"Good. I'm going back to sleep. See you in the kitchen at eight, for a real English breakfast."

He worked right up until eight. Then, after Fulvia left for the office with everything already prepared for the midday meal, he corrected, retyped and put all the pages in order; then he threw himself down on the bed, plunging at once into a leaden sleep.

He woke up in the early afternoon and immediately called Fulvia at the office.

"I've finished. I'm coming up to deliver the typescript to Mario. Tell him to wait for me."

"For heaven's sake, don't go anywhere. I'll be right there. I'll ask for the rest of the day off. Wait for me."

She turned to Mario. "Can I go?"

"Sure. Was that Fabrizio?"

"Yes, he's finished. Don't you go anywhere either," she said. "I think he'll be by soon to give you something."

She hurried off like a little red mother hen running to the aid of her chick.

Across the street the little chick gratefully awaited the arrival of the mother hen. She considered him entirely unversed in the ways of the world and capable of making a terrible deal even with his best friend; and she was right.

Fulvia was made of different stuff. Her moral toughness, her loyalty, her sincerity, her faithfulness to bargains, were absolute: there was never any question that she could look after herself and knew how to get what was coming to her. That was her style, the mark of the great, old, noble stock of Adelmo Basso, the cooper; it was something that could not be bought or taught—a system, a universe of objects, laws and memories so ingrained that it entered the blood and became second nature: a legacy, the only possession one could avail oneself of with genuine confidence, even with eyes closed, a cornerstone on which to build all subsequent constructions, a solid base to rest on or to take off from, a standard for relations with others and a model for solitude, a receptacle for one's beliefs, sustenance for one's desires.

Fabrizio was aware that he, like everyone else, had also been handed down a legacy, but something had wasted it, spoiled it. What remained for him had no value whatsoever; it was a burden, a source of oppression, not sustenance, and it left him defenceless against the world, full of admiration for the Basso clan and full of envious disdain for the triumphant mob of hustlers and imposters who, in their rush to succeed, had relinquished every bit of genuineness they had ever possessed and now masked their original indecency with the unreliable, uncomfortable, tight-fitting clothing they donned on gala occasions. He saw this mob as the slimy algae that slowly and inexorably take over dying seas. Mario was his only friend, and he trusted him; but Mario too was a little cog in the hated, all-powerful culture industry, inexhaustible progenetrix of the brood that Fabrizio detested most of all, almighty monster that had it in for him, that wanted him dead.

The important thing was to have his little warrior angel at his side. With her there he smelled the sweet fragrance of sawdust and saw the whole squad of coopers ready to back him up.

This was why he had humbly agreed to wait for her.

"All right," he had said, "I'm not going anywhere. I'll wait right here."

Fulvia arrived with a nice new folder for the typescript.

"You might as well present it properly," she said.

Fabrizio wanted only to obey her. He stood there watching her, full of admiration, as she gathered together the typewritten pages and put them into the folder. When she had finished, she took him by the hand and sat him down next to her on the sofa.

"Now listen closely to what I say," she said. "If not for you, this book would not even exist, right? It had vanished altogether, as though it had never been written. It's *yours*. It's not like all the other translations you've done, it's something else entirely, don't you agree?"

"Oh, yes. Something else entirely."

"Therefore, Mario *can't* give you the usual five or six thousand lire per page, right? You have to have a share in the book's fortunes, come what may; a share in the royalties—ask for ten percent. It wouldn't be right for you to ask for as much as they give the bigwigs, since you're not one, at least not yet. But you have to be the one to say it, don't wait for Mario to make an offer. Promise you'll do as I say?"

"I'm sure he'll suggest it himself."

"It might not occur to him. Had it occurred to you?"

"No, in fact."

"Well, then. For once, forget about shyness, restraint and

good breeding. That stuff's all well and good and I wouldn't want you any other way. But this is not the time for it. Promise?"

"Promise."

"One more thing," she said, stroking his cheek and looking at him tenderly.

"She's going to say something unpleasant," thought Fabrizio.

"It's something I've been wanting to ask you for a month. Why didn't you want to say anything to Mario before going off to Vienna, and why have you kept it all a secret until now?"

"Because I wanted to do it my own way, and I didn't want him meddling in my work," replied Fabrizio, looking away.

"That's nonsense. Mario has never meddled in your work. He wouldn't dare. He has a doglike reverence for your learning, your intelligence . . . Of course, he would never trust you to mail a postcard for him, and neither would I, for that matter . . . Come on, tell me the real reason behind all this mystery."

"The reason is that I was afraid. I was afraid that once the existence of the book came to be known, Mario—if he thought he could make a killing on it—would go off to look for it himself so he could give the job to some other translator, some fashionable Germanist like your friend Ribelli or some novelist who would come out with one of those 'creative' translations so full of imagination that *Wort* gets translated as 'wart.' "

Fulvia said nothing for a moment, then: "And what does *Wort* really mean?"

"Word."

"Look here," she said, getting up from the sofa and going over to the table, where she picked up the folder she had prepared and removed the photocopies of the original text that Fabrizio had made in Mondsee. "Don't give these to Mario. And don't tell him where you found the book. Just tell him it was all very difficult, and nothing more."

"I can't do that. It's not possible."

"Of course you can. Did you or did you not steal away to Austria like a thief? Why didn't you discuss it with him right away? Why didn't you go to Vienna together? Who created all this atmosphere of suspense, anyway? You started this game, now you must play it through to the end; when everything's been settled, you can tell him the whole story and then apologize."

Now that it had been suggested to him, all this sneakiness seemed abysmally petty. He realized with dismay how vast a distance there was between the terms of his friendship with Mario and the ridiculous behavior he had let himself fall into. But his shame barely lasted a minute before it was replaced by a wonderful feeling of relief; it was Fulvia who was now imposing this absurd wariness on him—he and Mario were once again the bosom buddies that they had always been, as inseparable as Siamese twins.

Much later, Mario asked Fulvia what her real intent had been in giving Fabrizio that bit of advice; had she hoped to provoke him—by counting on his irrepressible spirit of contradiction—into resuming normal relations with the rest of the world, starting with his best friend, or had she actually wanted to corroborate his feelings of mistrust to protect him from any eventual foul play?

Her staggering reply was "Both." But that was Fulvia, that was her way of reasoning—so versatile, so consistent with reality (and all its contradictions) that, blithely unaware of the basic principles of logic, she could hope through one action to achieve two opposite results, and not alternately, but simultaneously.

"I'll do as you say," replied Fabrizio. "Will you wait for me here? I'll only be a minute."

He arrived at Mario's office radiating friendliness, and anxious to talk.

"You'll see," he said, his handsome, boyish face smiling as he pranced around the office in a burst of euphoric energy.

"Once you've read it, and once I've told you how it all happened, you'll see. It was a miracle from beginning to end." He was still keeping his secret, but no longer out of mistrust; now he wanted to surprise Mario, to astonish him.

Fulvia was waiting for him when he returned.

"I'm going out for a walk," he said to her. "Come, I'll walk downstairs with you."

"I was thinking of putting the dishes away."

"Don't bother. The maid is coming tomorrow."

They went downstairs together and stopped in front of the building.

"Which way are you headed?" asked Fabrizio. "Are you going straight home or back to the office?"

"I'm going to stop by the office for a minute . . . Well, I guess you're finished now."

"Thank God. Maybe I'll ask my sister to give me the keys to her house in Maremma for a few days."

"All right. Well, good-bye."

"Good-bye. And thanks so much for all your kindness. You really were a big help."

He wandered aimlessly through the city's streets until the stores began to close. He lingered a long time in front of windows displaying the latest in recording gadgetry.

He knew that by now Mario had already begun reading *Das Haus am Mondsee* and was positive he would love it. He felt satisfied and full of hope.

All the while he had been working on the translation, time had been suspended, and with it all his fears, misgivings and resentments. Around him, weeks had passed, things had happened, some of which had been judged important enough to be recorded and commented upon by the newspapers. Closer to home, Fulvia had hurried about carrying grocery bags, cooking, keeping him company at meals, keeping him warm at night. But she too, like the days rolling by and the things happening in the world outside, had remained a bit out of focus.

Fabrizio had lived through those five weeks immersed in the same sort of thick fog that cloaks the minds of those ghostlike adolescents whom one sees sliding through cities on roller skates, cut off from the rest of humanity by a difference of speed—that small gap across which it becomes impossible for two people to look each other in the eye and acknowledge each other—and by the cocoon of sound created by the earphones attached to the little music boxes on their chests.

Now that the work was over, the wave of space and time had recaptured him, gently setting him down for the moment on a tiny little island before hurling him into new and darker depths.

Part II

MARIA

$$\text{———— } 12 \text{ ————}$$

FULVIA HAD NOT gone back to the office after she and Fabrizio parted company in front of his apartment building. She had gone back upstairs, packed her bags and left.

The extra set of keys lay on the coffee table in the living room. Her half of the closet was empty. Fabrizio didn't know whether to feel relieved or upset. The fact that Fulvia had to leave, and as soon as possible, was one of those things that he would neither say nor deny, but that he had had every intention of bringing about, in one manner or another, even though he could not literally put her out. He was too much of a gentleman for that.

Why, then, wasn't he glad that she had taken the hint all by herself? Perhaps it left a slightly bitter taste in his mouth, as if she had *wanted* to leave?

No, it wasn't nearly as simple as that. The empty closet and the keys on the table constituted a clear message—since, after all, they bore Fulvia's signature. There was nothing ambiguous about them, nothing that might later be denied with a straight face. Like everything she did, they represented a conscious, binding act. And since this matter also concerned him and the future of their relations, he would once again have to face obstacles and choices for which he was not cut out: straight lines, perpendicular planes—either here or there, yes or no.

He had foreseen a much more natural solution: within a few days' time they would have quarreled, as they often did, and Fulvia, no longer held back by her promise to help him out while he was working on the translation, would have packed up and left. But their quarrels never lasted very long, and soon everything would have gone back to the way it was before—that is, each in his own house, with no obligations, commitments or deadlines.

In arranging this scenario—which was not a precise plan but merely a hypothetical eventuality that he would have let himself fall into if and when the moment came—he had neglected to take into account Fulvia's adamant nature, her inability to sink into the featherbed of ill-defined circumstances, her lack of appreciation for soft outlines. But it was probably nothing serious. He just had to leave her alone for a few days, then call her as though nothing had happened.

After having packed her suitcases and put her keys on the table, Fulvia had crossed the street and gone back to the office. Mario was reading Fabrizio's manuscript.

"It's good, isn't it?" she asked.

"It's beautiful."

"So you're going to publish it."

"Of course. It's a real find, a coup."

"I'm so happy!" Fulvia shouted, bursting into tears.

Mario jumped up at once and took her in his arms.

"Darling," he babbled, "baby . . . What's wrong?"

"This time it's over for good," she sobbed. "He didn't send me away or anything—I mean, he didn't say or do anything to make me leave; but he didn't reassure me either; he didn't say, 'Well, what do you think we should do now?'; he didn't even say, 'You're very sweet, but I was born to live alone' or

'It just won't work between the two of us . . .' He's exactly the same as before . . . He's finally accomplished something, something important; he's finally gotten over what I considered his handicap, the thing that always enabled me to forgive him for everything, and he hasn't changed a bit! Do you want to know what I think about all this? Do you want to know what kind of wild ideas I've been carrying around inside me since I was twenty? I happen to believe that if a man and a woman love each other, they should share the same food and live under the same roof—and they should have children, if they can and if it's not too late; and for as long as their love endures—forever, if they're lucky—they should make a commitment to serve it, they should give it a name, a background. Do you know what I mean? And you know what else I sometimes wish? I wish I could be the mistress of one of those distinguished gentlemen who firmly believe in the sacred bond of marriage and strengthen this faith through the comforts of adultery; someone—one of those men who is all home, work and family—who could grant me the assurance of knowing that as long as I knew how to make him happy, he would come and see me every Wednesday, come what may, with a box of marrons glacés or a Gucci purse; of knowing that, though I could never, of course, call him at home or at work, there was a secret code I could use in emergencies to let him know I needed him, and that I could count on him to answer my call at once. At least there would be some kind of law between us, however sordid, hypocritical and dishonest toward everyone involved, a commitment that would give meaning to our actions and our days—instead of this constant neglect, this permanent uncertainty . . ."

She clutched at his neck like a little girl.

"Can I sleep on your couch tonight?"

"Of course, my dear. But I still don't really understand what that miserable cad did to you."

He led her over to the couch she had just invoked and sat down next to her without releasing his embrace. He felt as though he had attained a position very close to happiness, and he would have liked not to say or think of anything, for fear of somehow losing his prized place. But there still were all those things that Fabrizio did or didn't do, did or didn't say, which seemed to be so important. He had to get to the bottom of it all.

"Just tell me, in brief, what that imbecile did," he repeated. "What he did that was different from usual, that makes it impossible for you to forgive him this time. Can you do that?"

"But he didn't do anything different. This book meant so much to him. I'm the one who got it all wrong. From the moment he started working on it, letting me read every night the pages he had translated that day, I had gotten it into my head that something so beautiful and so much his own— because it really is his, you know . . . I mean, it took someone like him to find it, someone who can rummage through a book- stall with the kind of confidence he has with books, someone who sees things that pass everyone else by, who, when he reads the words 'an original, successful invention that is both surprising and convincing,' has a little bell that goes off inside his head—anyway, I had gotten this idea that since he was the only person in the world cut out for this project and had done such a good job with it, I had gotten the idea that this book— which isn't his own in fact but really is, in a way—could become his backbone, just like that, overnight . . . But what actually happened was that I came to realize, overnight, that he would never have a backbone, that he would never be able to face what you, I think, once called 'the test of two'—and so to hell with it all."

"I see," said Mario.

"Well, I'm glad you do, because if I were to tell you the things about Fabrizio that really make me see red, if I were to list them one by one, you'd never understand. You'd think I was crazy. How can I possibly explain to anyone, even to you, who are such a dear friend, how insulted I feel at the fact that he never uses the first person plural when talking about the future? How can anyone take such a dry grammatical accusation seriously?"

"I am always ready to take you seriously," bellowed Mario, "but this time you've really lost me."

"He never says, for example, 'when we are old'; he says 'when I am old' or 'when you are old'; he doesn't even say, for example, 'When Marilyn Horne comes to town to sing in *Tancredi* next week, we really must go see her'; he says, 'When Marilyn Horne comes to town next week to sing in *Tancredi*, I don't want to miss it.' "

"I get it. Yet in fact, when Marilyn Horne was here, you went to La Scala together."

"Of course. And as far as he's concerned we'll grow old together too. I'm the one who's fed up with this way of doing things. I need a commitment, remember? Maybe others can scrape along till they drop dead, if that's the way it's done these days, but I don't want any more of it."

"Why don't you say these things to him?"

"Because it's not possible. He would jump ten feet in the air, grab on to the chandelier and refuse to come down until I had left the province. When he's afraid he doesn't reason or respond, he becomes mean, disloyal and dishonest. He'll do anything just to avoid being put to the test. He's afraid of me because we love each other, and there's no test that fills him with more horror than this—the 'test of two,' as you once put it so well, aging bachelor that you are."

She wasn't crying anymore and in fact seemed much less unhappy than before.

They had dinner together.

"You know I'm in love with you, don't you?" Mario said to her later.

"Yes, I know. And you no doubt know that I don't console myself by eating candy or signing up for yoga courses. Is that what you were thinking of?"

"No. I mean yes, maybe. I don't know. I'm here, in any case."

"With you it's different. If I were to go to bed with you now, it would harm your friendship with Fabrizio. We have to be wise and patient, like two old camels. And now let's not think about it anymore."

Mario did not sleep a wink all night, on account of the excitement of having Fulvia there in his house and the hope of conquering her sooner or later; but he was also troubled because Fabrizio's preface was hopelessly bad and he didn't know how he was going to tell him this when he saw him in the morning. As he kept reading and rereading it through the night, it seemed more and more muddled and inane, yet he couldn't quite figure out where it went wrong. Only much later did he realize that it resembled an author's introduction to his own work. It had that deliberately modest tone that deep down smacks of self-satisfaction and is almost always a disaster, even when it actually is the author who is presenting his own work. In this instance, with Fabrizio introducing Oberhofer, the effect was downright ridiculous.

The next morning, when Mario called Fabrizio to ask him to come by so they could discuss the book, Fulvia, in order to avoid him, decided to go out to take care of some of the endless bureaucratic chores that even a company as small as theirs had to contend with.

"So you've read the whole thing? What do you think?" she asked before going out.

"Fantastic. The preface, however, is awful."

"But you're going to publish it anyway, aren't you?"

"No. I thought about it all night and decided I can't. Just the novel."

"Poor thing. He had so much trouble writing it. It just wouldn't come to him."

"Well, it never did come, I'm afraid."

"Go easy on him. Try not to hurt his feelings."

Her eyes were full of tenderness. Mario felt more jealous

because of that look than he had felt in the entire two years since he'd first met Fulvia.

"Have you already changed your mind? You're going to take your little weasel back?"

"That's the furthest thing from my mind." She gave him a kiss that seemed more promising than their usual chaste exchanges of affection and went out.

Mario worked for love, but also for money; he was ready to bet his shirt on *Das Haus am Mondsee*, and he did not want, even for the sake of friendship, to spoil the book with a bad preface.

But he did not like what he was about to do to Fabrizio. And the plans he was hatching with regard to Fulvia further aggravated his feeling of uneasiness. All throughout his conversation with Fabrizio, horrified at his own behavior but unable to act otherwise, he demonstrated an unctuous politeness that to his own nose smelled of betrayal.

He began by greeting him with open arms, in an airy display of excessive cordiality.

"My dear Fabrizio, come in, sit down. You have brought me a gem. I simply couldn't put the book down until I had read it all. Sit down, sit down. I'm going to publish it immediately—I'll set everything else aside for the moment—so I can give it all the attention it deserves."

Fabrizio sat down, looking at him in mild amazement. Their usual manner of relating was much more blunt, ironic, informal.

"I'm going to do everything I can to ensure its success," continued Mario.

"Widespread promotion and all the rest?"

"Of course, of course . . . With no holds barred!"

"I want ten percent on all sales . . . and an immediate advance if possible, seeing that I'm flat broke and still owe half a million lire to Fulvia."

"By all means! It's only fair."

"Then let's draw up the contract right now."

"Wait. Let's think for a minute. I have promised you ten percent. We have to do this thing right. It's in your interest too that the book sell well."

"I should think so."

"Right." He got up from his armchair, circled the desk and went up to Fabrizio. He put a hand on his shoulder and leaned down until his lips brushed Fabrizio's ear.

"You have made a great discovery," he whispered ."A sensational discovery. We have to give it all the backing we can, so it will soar as high as possible. We have to get a big shot, a heavyweight, to do the preface."

"What, you want to have two prefaces?"

"No, no, just one."

"What about mine?"

"Yours we'll put aside for the moment. We'll take its main points and make the jacket copy from it. Trust me, an introduction by an illustrious Germanist is essential."

Not even wise old Fulvia had prepared him for this. Fabrizio felt himself sinking into that familiar, anguished torment of his, that of finding himself in an unexpected situation, caught completely off guard, with no appropriate reaction. With a great deal of effort—swallowing hard and holding his head high—he managed to control his tears. They did, all the same, cover his eyes with a shiny, doleful film but at least did not spill over to the point of running down his cheeks, as with a child.

"I was hoping that *I* would become an illustrious Germanist . . . with this very book." He bit his lip. Oh, God, he had let himself get carried away like a fool. His voice had quavered, wet with all the tears he was holding back.

"Listen," said Mario. "We'll have Trifani himself, the best of them all, do the critical introduction . . . And we'll also have him tell the story of the book's discovery. He'll praise you in a way that you could never do yourself . . ."

He really did feel for Fabrizio. He looked like an adolescent sitting there, so thin, his hair falling down onto his forehead— a Saint Sebastian with moist eyes gazing skyward, a resigned suffering trembling on his handsome, delicate face. He was his best friend, in whom all the world's fortunes and misfortunes were embodied, so pathetic in many respects and yet—and this was the quality that most touched Mario at that moment— so diligent, conscientious and punctual, especially in his work, which he did for little money and no acclaim, as though in expiation of some ancient sin; his dear old slogger, from whom he was now plotting to steal Fulvia.

"But you'll get your chance to become a famous Germanist, because there's something else I want from you."

The idea had flashed through his mind just then, as a way to give Fabrizio a break; but as it was taking shape in his head it began to seem like an excellent idea, even from a practical point of view. The major books—so to speak—that he published all came out in the same relatively expensive format. Then there was the little subseries, the "Satellites," which were simpler in format, made of more modest materials and which cost considerably less. They were slim little books, usually rather short, and, as the name implied, each revolved around one of the books in the main series.

"You already have enough material for it," he said, "but why don't you go back to Austria, at my expense, and write a short biography of Fritz Oberhofer? About a hundred pages— ninety, a hundred and ten. How old did you say he was when he died, thirty-eight?"

"Yes."

"Perfect. We'll bring the book out in the Satellite series, three weeks after the novel. A book all your own—what do you say?"

If the novel was successful, as he firmly believed it would be, the biography would also fare well. And who could be better for the job than Fabrizio, who seemed to be the only person on earth who knew of the forgotten writer's existence?

"Well? Do you like the idea?"

Fabrizio was anxious to appear tough and indifferent, to make his friend forget his moment of abandon.

"Well, as far as I'm concerned . . . I have, as you can imagine, all the material, really . . . The biography's already written, in a way."

It was even true, he thought, as it was also true that it would be a book all his own—FABRIZIO GARRONE, and below, something like *The Short Life of Fritz Oberhofer.*

"I'll go back to Austria just to have a look at some rococo at your expense, and to gather a few last details . . . By when do you need the job done?"

"It has to be ready a month from today. But I'll tell you now that I'm going to put this in the contract as a mandatory deadline. The novel has to come out right away, before someone else tracks it down . . ."

"That, I assure you, is very unlikely."

"We have to be cautious. And the biography has to come out in the wake of the interest aroused by the novel. Otherwise, who's going to read it? Therefore, be punctual, or the deal's off."

He pulled him out of his chair, embraced him and then began to push him toward the door.

"Eighty, a hundred pages, no more," he repeated. "Don't bother to analyze his work; just tell the story of his life. How old did you say he was when he died?"

"Thirty-eight."

"Perfect."

Now Fabrizio could phone Fulvia. He would tell her about the agreement he had made with Mario and give her back the money she had lent him. No explanations, no reconciliations. The normal rhythm of their relationship would resume the day he left for Austria, and both the month spent living together and the day of silence and separation would fall away, cut out of time, without consequence or sequel. Things that had already happened could enter the present only through words, or so Fabrizio thought; indeed, often it was actually the present which—if one was clever enough—entered the past, erasing it with silence.

Having noticed that Fulvia was not at the office, he tried calling her at home but got no answer. He waited fifteen minutes, then began calling Mario. Three times Mario told him—lying, at Fulvia's request, the last two times—that she wasn't there and would not be in for the rest of the day.

He tried her again at home, a bit before eight, hoping to invite her to dinner; but she, at that very moment, was in Mario's kitchen making a risotto.

He finally got hold of her at the office the following morning, when Mario had stepped out and she had no choice but to answer the telephone.

"Darling Fulvia, I'm sure Mario has already told you everything, but I still want to tell you the news myself." His voice issued from his chest like an oily liquid, opaque and slippery.

She showed interest in what he had to say and expressed delight at his good fortune.

He went on and on. When he was finally done, he said: "If you join me for dinner tonight, I can give you back the dough."

"You'll have to leave it downstairs with the concierge. Tonight I'm busy and tomorrow I'm off to spend the weekend at home."

"Wonderful! Have fun, and give my regards to the family . . . By the way, I have to go back to Austria very soon, probably Monday or Tuesday. How would you feel about coming with me?"

"No, thank you."

"NO, THANK YOU."

Thus did Mother, with a slight nod of her little blond head above her delicate neck, and an even slighter smile playing at the tip of her lips—for her lips, in certain instances, had a tip like the point of a razor-sharp pencil drawing invisible pictures —dismiss the butler and his tray of canapés: an exquisite touch of formal gratitude toward the gesture of offering, but only a touch, since Angelo, after all, merely did what he was paid to do.

Fulvia's "no, thank you" had suddenly brought back to mind that other, distant "no, thank you." A toneless utterance politely refusing a meaningless offer. The people in the house at the end of the garden, when they went into their sky-blue kitchen with Mario for a midafternoon snack of bread and tomatoes, put more feeling into their offers, acceptances and refusals of food: for them, who had no lighter, more transparent means of expression, food was a token of love.

But the lady of the pink house said "no, thank you," barely nodding her precious little head and smiling with the tip of her lips. Lacking appetite since adolescence, she was possessed of the same age-old satiety as fat Aunt Irene (sitting at the piano with the keyboard closed and a full plate on top) and everyone else gathered in that bright, lovely room that day.

The French windows facing the garden's first terrace are filled with sunlight, for the thuja—the biggest ever seen— stands a bit to the east, on the first step of an immense stair- case that leads past the magnolia gardens, the rose gardens, the greenhouses, the city's slate rooftops, the port and the light- house, all the way down to the sea.

It is sometime around 1950. Teodora—in her canary-yellow crepe dress and her white cotton kneesocks—and little Fabrizio are invited in to tea, but only for a few minutes, just to say hello and receive a kiss or two, which fall from on high, borne by a little-known face, and then it's off again with the Fräulein. Mario, too, is there, avid and curious, but only in spirit, his mortal frame not welcomed in those parlors until much later, when Teodora was already at the university and invited him to her receptions.

The brickwork floors, the braids of garlic, the stone fireplace are still where they have always been, like the calloused hands, the smells of bleach and cabbages, the rope-soled shoes.

But in that drawing room of soft beige and lavender, the furniture is *haute époque* and nourishment a distracted pursuit devoid of sentimental, cultural or moral significance, even when, as with Aunt Irene, eating is a loathsome vice. For these people, centuries of plenty have stripped food of its sacred- ness; TV and magazines have not yet intervened to give it back. And to the lady of that salon, it would make no differ- ence even when they did: she was more attuned to the cen- turies than to television or magazines.

"No, thank you." (Politeness, aloofness, simplicity: all in very small doses, light as watercolor hues.)

"No, thank you," Fulvia had said.

She had not said it to make him insist, to drag him into a quarrel—with the usual reproaches, demands and that self- righteous demeanor she felt entitled to wear like a suit of silver armor. For although she was indeed unfaithful to him every time he let her down, it was never she who let him down. She considered herself reliable, affectionate, sincere, obliging, energetic, loyal; and she was right. Fabrizio she saw as evasive, surly, deceitful, egotistical, devious; and here, too, she was right. And she never failed, whenever they fought, to present herself implicitly as an example, which was the very thing that sent him into a rage.

An old story. This time she didn't want to quarrel. The "no, thank you" that had tinkled in the receiver like a splinter of ice, reviving an echo of that faraway watercolor voice, meant simply "no, thank you" and nothing more. Fulvia never minced words. Her words and tone were to be taken at face value, without interpretations. She did not want to see him, she did not want to go to Austria with him, she did not want there to be anything more between them. There was no point in wondering whether this resolve arose from a moment's passion or a reasoned decision, because decisions were the very passion of that little warrior angel and her passions were decisive.

Fabrizio was at a loss. What had *he* done wrong? She had come on her own initiative, and had left on her own initiative. She had told him "I'll stay with you until you've finished," and that was exactly what she had done. What did he have to do with it? To hell with her.

"As you wish. I'll call when I get back."

This time, he decided, he could go by plane, at Mario's expense. He would skip Vienna and go directly to Mondsee, since everything that could possibly be gathered about Fritz's life up to 1910 was now contained in his file, which he had put back in his suitcase with the intention of starting the biography while still in Austria.

Fritz was so transparently autobiographical in all his novels that he would serve as Fabrizio's personal guide in putting all his documents in order. Like the others, *Das Haus am Mondsee* also told a true story, the story of the adolescent Fritz's love for a forty-year-old married woman. Fabrizio had already identified the woman—a friend of Aunt Lieselotte—as well as the story's real setting: a little house in Grinzing where the seventeen-year-old lover raced every day on his bicycle when the woman's husband was away on business involving his position in the Imperial government.

Thus in addition to the woman's name, Fritz had changed the story's setting—no doubt for the sake of discretion, but also, perhaps, because he wanted to set the novel amid the landscape that he saw all around him as he was writing, since those surroundings were, after all, inspirational and must have kindled his love and filled him with gratitude.

Fabrizio was sure of it; the plot of *Das Haus am Mondsee* was remote in time, but its landscape was present—it was right there, where Fritz had chosen to spend his retreat, to write his masterpiece. And it was there, on the little lake near Salzburg, that Fabrizio would find the last three years of the writer's life.

It was a plausible lead, but more important, it was the only one he had. The house where Fritz had come to live in 1910, and where he died in 1913, *had* to be one of those around the Mondsee. During those three years, he had loved a woman; more than this, Fabrizio did not know.

Now that he was on official assignment and had enough money for his purposes, he could throw caution to the wind and conduct his search openly, asking all the questions he needed.

First he had to go back to the guesthouse where he had unearthed the book. He had no doubt he could find it again, even though it hadn't occurred to him to write down the hotel's name and address. But when the bus dropped him off in the town this time, the place looked so incredibly different from his first visit that he couldn't get his bearings.

The dead winter calm had given birth to a ghastly flowering

of miniature golf courses, swimming pools and windsurfing schools, all of them teeming with crass, noisy vacationers. At the tourist office he asked for the names of all the hotels along the lake and found that there were far more than he had imagined, a virtual infinity. Undaunted, he asked for the list and rented a bicycle with the intention of checking out every last one of them.

He took a room—the only vacant one he could find—in a hotel on the square in front of the church. He reconfirmed that Oberhofer, Friedrich had in fact died in 1913, of pneumonia, at the age of thirty-eight, within the town limits of Mondsee. He found Oberhofer's grave in the old part of the cemetery. Then he began his explorations. He spent afternoons and evenings writing the first part of Fritz Oberhofer's biography with the help of the documents he had gathered in Vienna; mornings, he took the bicycle and went off in search of those three lost years.

He went around questioning the old people of the town: the parish priest, the owner of the hunting and fishing supply store, the ancient director of the Castle Disco, who had been a waiter there when the same locale housed a small elegant restaurant.

None of them knew anything about the young Viennese who had come there seventy years before to write a masterpiece and to love a woman. His presence apparently had not aroused curiosity nor did it provoke the kind of gossip that might have remained etched in the memories of those who were still small children at the time.

Fabrizio's only hope was to find the hotel on the lake, the one with the stuffed fish; the more it began to seem that some absurd spell had hidden that place from him, the more convinced he felt that everything would be resolved once he found it.

From time to time he would call Milan, hoping to talk to Fulvia. But each time, as soon as she heard his voice, she would say "Hi, here's Mario." Then Mario would keep the conversation going for five minutes or so, telling him the latest news of Milan, asking him questions, making jokes. It worked because he had, in fact, nothing to hide, much to his regret. Fulvia, once she had gotten over the first anguished days of her painful decision, had gone back to sleeping at her own apartment and started going out with an economist from the Catholic University. Mario, however, had not given up hope; he felt that, given the nature of his feelings for Fabrizio, Fulvia saw it as only proper to avoid creating strife by jumping directly from his friend's bed into his bed. He tried very hard to consider the economist—and any subsequent lovers—as mere insulation, simple Styrofoam not worth brooding or losing sleep over.

"How far along are you?" he asked Fabrizio.

"I'm almost finished. Everything's going fine."

And in fact, during the hours he spent writing, especially at night, he felt that Fritz was there with him, assisting him in his impassioned task of bringing him back to life. The pages filled up all by themselves, more effortlessly each day, as though he were content to go along with the bizarre fantasy— which took hold of him after the night had silenced the din of the tourists—that it was he himself telling his own story, beginning with early childhood; his grandfather's death in the beautiful villa at Neustift am Walde, first prize in Greek at grammar school, the lady in Grinzing, the flight with Tilly, the evenings at the Café Griensteidl with friends, with the distinguished members of Jung Wien, the Burgtheater, the Staatsoper.

He would sit in that clean, anonymous room, so seemingly ill-suited to the summoning of mysterious presences, and submissively let himself be permeated and possessed by the Other.

The Other, however, would leave him to his own devices when he went off on his two-wheeled excursions. But it didn't matter, for during those moments Fabrizio was not looking for Fritz, the amiable phantom who so obligingly let himself be called forth, rising up not only from the documents but as though from the very depths of Fabrizio's own memory—he was looking for her, the peerless last mistress, who seventy years earlier had come into Fritz's life bearing the gift of poetry. But she resisted him, fled his pursuit. In those moments, nothing was easy; it was merely a question of stubbornness or goodwill, but all he got for his efforts were feelings of discouragement and frustration.

Fabrizio was nevertheless certain he would find the unknown woman the very moment he set foot again in that elusive guesthouse, that she would jump right out of the past exactly as she was then, ready to hand him the key to the secret. And this certainty, together with his delicious anticipation of the work that awaited him each evening, gave him strength.

He tried not to think about Fulvia; the possibility of having lost her forever filled him with dread; but he was even more terrified at the thought of the things he would have to do, the words he would have to pronounce in order to bring her back to him. He knew that those words and actions would have to possess the sort of clarity that he shunned as though it were a foreign, hostile element in which he could not survive.

The day came when the biography of Fritz Oberhofer, from his birth until 1910, was completed—written, revised, retyped. The friendly presence had finally received his tribute and now lay quietly in his tomb of heavy-duty cardboard.

Fabrizio was left alone with his bicycle.

The following morning he resumed his quest more downcast than usual; that was the day he found the old guesthouse again.

There was the landlady in her dirndl—light blue this time, with an apron dotted with little red flowers—and there was the glass showcase, the fish with the sinister grin, the photo of Franz Lehar, the rifle, the silver cup; but the book was gone.

"Yes, I remember," said the woman. "You stayed here a while ago and asked to see the book . . . Are you sure you returned it?"

"Why, of course!"

"Yes, come to think of it, I remember myself . . . But then where could I have put it? In its usual place I guess, but how strange that it's not there anymore . . . Why would anyone want to take it?"

"Is the showcase locked?"

"Oh, no, who would want to steal anything from there? Especially an old book . . . It looks like I probably threw it away myself . . . One thing is certain, it's no longer there; *Es tut mir Leid*. Do you need it?"

"Well, yes and no. What I need most is to know what happened to the author between 1910 and 1913, because he was living here during that time."

"At this hotel?"

"No, no, in Mondsee, I mean . . . But, who knows, perhaps yes, perhaps at this very hotel, if it already existed . . ."

"Oh, it did indeed, and long before that too. But you can't expect me to know anything about a client who stayed with us twenty years before I was born! Now if my father were still alive, or better yet my grandfather . . ."

It was the high season and there was much work to be done. This young man was wasting her time. He was different from the way she remembered him. He was still thin, though before this had seemed to suggest a fiery disposition, a manly flame that burned away all excess softness; now his thinness made her think of something sick, of some pale, viscid parasite eating away at him.

"I'll get you the gardener, he's the oldest person here."

The gardener didn't know a thing. His position was hereditary, and in 1910 he was already living at the hotel, in the same little house by the pier. But he was only six years old at the time and could remember nothing about any of the clients who came and went. *Es tut mir Leid.*

Fabrizio's search ended there. There was nothing left to do but to go back to Milan. And leave the last three years blank? He couldn't. He had to find a solution.

$$——— 14 ———$$

AS SOON AS FABRIZIO arrived home he called the office looking for Fulvia, but she had already left for her vacation. He felt abandoned, but also a bit relieved. This way, everything was postponed; no fateful "no's" would be pronounced. She would probably just reappear one day of her own accord, golden-brown from the sun, a bit contrite (since she certainly hadn't gone away alone), her anger subsided, as pleasant and affectionate as ever.

He told Mario he had just about finished the book. In another week it would be ready.

"In the meantime I'll give you the first part. There are only about twenty more pages to go."

"Fine, but don't waste any time. *The House on Moon Lake* will be in the bookstores this Monday. It's already much-awaited; you have no idea how much commotion we've stirred up. The biography has to come out at the best possible moment; I'm giving you exactly eight days to finish the book. Hole up in your apartment and get busy."

If Fabrizio had any sort of literary mastery of intangibles—of "ifs" and "maybes"—he might have been able to create a certain effect with those three lost years, three years of inspiration and love, vanished without a trace. Yet as hard as he tried to do this, he was always left with an incomplete biography that seemed negligent, like a work left unfinished.

His mystical certainty of finding the reward for his efforts at the guesthouse on the lake had dissolved into disillusionment, opening wider than ever the wound of his distrust, his dark conviction of being the only creature on earth from whom all was taken away and nothing returned.

Thus he did not ask Mario's advice, and they did not resolve the matter together.

If he had been able to return Fulvia's love in kind, he would have her at his side now to help him. As things stood, all he could do was convince himself that the only way to resolve the problem was to invent everything, and to do so in the greatest of secrecy.

He would have Fritz live in the guesthouse by the lake, where he had found the book. Fritz's days would be very much like Fabrizio's days writing the biography: cycling excursions in the morning, an occasional boat ride, afternoons at the worktable. The landscape would be the same as he had glimpsed it on his first visit to Mondsee: no saunas, no miniature golf courses, no tourists—just a splendid, humble tableau of orderly, industrious simplicity.

The problems arose when it came to finding a sweetheart for Fritz. Though *The House on Moon Lake* was of course a love story, the teenage Fritz's adventure with the lady from Grinzing clearly had nothing to do with the living emotions that the thirty-five-year-old author was experiencing at the time of writing the book. Fabrizio could not draw inspiration for his forgery from the novel's heroine. One thing he was sure of, however, was that if Fritz Oberhofer's last love was another one of those full, rich, glowing experiences that seemed always to befall him, this could only mean that he had once again come upon that absolute rarity among creatures, a lovable woman.

An absolute rarity. Fabrizio himself was not at all favorably disposed to women at that moment, what with Fulvia having gone off who-knows-where with who-knows-whom, leaving him tottering between the desolate prospect of loneliness and the panic that seized him every time his hope was revived and he remembered the proceedings he would have to set in motion if he wanted to appeal his case.

An absolute rarity. Not a refined, egotistical spectre like his mother, not a little strumpet in love with her own goodness such as Fulvia, nor any of the other women he had known, all of them immensely seductive from a distance and all of them insufferable as soon as they got close to him.

The day after his return he was invited to a dinner party that he knew would be attended by many people. As usual, he accepted, but this time he finally had a reason for going. Knowing he would find himself in the midst of many women after so long a period of seclusion, he resolved to study them, spy on them, imagine them in the intimacy of a day-to-day relationship and then take the best qualities of each and fuse them into a creature who could provide joy and happiness instead of merely inflicting boredom or pain or, worse yet— something not unfamiliar to him—both at the same time. That evening he did not suffer from his usual inability to take part in conversation. He amused himself; under the unsuspecting eyes of husbands and lovers, he was living out long, imaginary affairs with their women. And his pleasure lay not only in that secret game of infidelity into which he drew them unawares; there was an infidelity within the infidelity as well, for these women were in turn deceived by him, since in reality, under the guise of courtship, he was studying them with the cold detachment of an entomologist, only to hand them back to their husbands and lovers, annoyed and disappointed by them all: this one won't do, nor this one, nor this one . . .

He drank quite a lot that night, and had a little trouble walking when it came time to go home. Mario practically had to carry him up to the door of his apartment, and imagined he would collapse on his bed once inside, probably with all his clothes on. Too bad, he thought, that's his problem. Mario was in favor of moderation and had little tolerance for excess.

Once his friend had left, however, Fabrizio began pacing back and forth in his study, grim, reeling and bloated with hostility. His little collage of women, which had seemed so amusing when he was playing the game, had not worked out: those women were idiots, every last one of them. He had not been able to discern anything even remotely lovable in any of them.

He didn't want to go to bed because he had decided earlier to begin constructing his heroine that very night. Around dawn, at the first sound of blackbirds singing, he thought he saw a glimmer of hope. The solution: He would adopt, like Michelangelo, the method of *in cavare*, or "cutting away." Those silly girls, with their total lack of virtue, had inspired him after all.

He would imagine the abstract essence of womanhood as a large block of marble; from that block of marble he would chip away, blow by blow, all the women he had ever known, leaving behind, in the end, the one he was seeking, the truly lovable woman, the last sublime love of Fritz Oberhofer.

He turned to Saint Jerome—still blissful in his little study that lacked for nothing—and said aloud, "Do you think the approach is a bit mechanical?"

Saint Jerome did not answer, even though he seemed to have all around him the answer to every possible question. But Fabrizio had no need for answers. There really was nothing more to worry about. After all, it was only a matter of putting the last touches on a fine and, for the most part, finished work.

The demolition went swiftly, but it did not turn out as he had hoped. It went on for the entire day after his night of drinking, and when it was all over there was nothing left. After having struck away the images of all the women he had ever known, from his mother to Fulvia, he was back at square one with his character, except for the last name, Lettner—which he had chosen because he remembered that it was one of the most common in Mondsee—and the first name: Maria, of course.

A name was at least a start. And this wasn't one of those novelistic names that sound false, made up. It had an authentic ring to it: Maria Lettner. He had to make something grow out of that name . . . yes, that was it, *grow* out of it, as in nature; to make something sprout, spring up . . .

He began to write, keeping his mind on the honeysuckle bush that grew beside the thuja in the garden in Genoa; he thought of its winding shape, its cream-colored flowers, its fragrance and the quality that, in botany, described this type of plant: voluble.

Voluble. The word's ambiguity entranced him. Botanists define voluble plants as those whose shoots grow upward in a twining spiral—each species in its own way, the dextrorse twining only in a clockwise direction, the sinistrorse always in a counterclockwise direction; they are plants that embrace, clasp, cling to every branch, pole, gate they encounter in the path of their growth, interlocking with it for the rest of their days. Ivy, which is a climbing plant and not voluble, seems unworthy of its fame when compared to the unflaggingly tenacious wisteria, morning glory or honeysuckle.

Voluble, in botany, thus means the opposite of what we usually take the word to mean in common speech . . . Carried by the wave of enchantment that this contradiction stirred up in him, Fabrizio began to create Maria Lettner; and as he wrote he looked for models outside the human realm, in which he always felt so out of place.

He thought of certain stones—the smooth pebbles he had gathered from a stream in Val Gardena as a child, one of them gray with a thin white line running all around it, right at the equator, another one oval in shape and very black, so that it shone like licorice when wet. He thought of trees, flowers, mushrooms and birds, bearing in mind their colors, shapes, characters—and especially their names.

Thus Maria was *Laurus nobilis, Angelica Archangelica*; and yet at times she could be terrible, tempestuous—*Sturmschwalbe, Procellaria Gravis, Potentilla Tormentilla*. She was strong and courageous, someone in whom you could have faith: Kingfisher, Golden Eagle and even Levant Sparrow Hawk (who knows, perhaps a drop of Semitic blood—from this name he derived her nose, her demeanor and her unfathomable, disturbing psychological depth).

Then there was that special grace in the way she moved her hands, and in the delicate curve of her neck: *Demoiselle, Nigella damascena, Belladonna Lily*. She was also sweet and childish, almost silly at times: Willow Tit, Kittiwake, Peewit and Puffin.

Suddenly she needed to be sheltered, protected: *Campanula fragilis, Erica gracilis*. But she was also the Little Owl, who in Latin became *Athena Noctua*; and here Maria revealed yet another aspect, silvery and nocturnal—*Lunaria Perennis, Silene pendula*. In the sun, her chestnut hair blazed fire-red: *Russula Aurata*. And of course Cattleya, *ça va sans dire*, but also *Narcissus poeticus*.

He completed his portrait à la Arcimboldi after six days of passionate, loving labor, just in time to turn in the biography at the deadline.

———— 15 ————

WHEN *The House on Moon Lake* appeared, it created an un-
paralleled stir. Mario had made every effort to launch it
properly, pouring all his money into conventional advertising
for the first time since he had started his business, but also
and above all devoting himself body and soul to the more
personal, homespun kind of promotion he had always relied
on. The rumour-mill designed to arouse interest had been set
in motion with Teodora, as usual, in charge of the general
public. As for the specialists, he had lent the galley proofs to
a young critic who was not yet famous but all in all an intelligent and zealous professional. Indeed, they had had to restrain
him so that he would not get too carried away in his enthusiasm and say too much too soon.

Fulvia had been working behind the scenes, though officially
still on vacation. When she learned that Fabrizio had stopped
asking for her at the office, she went back to work, as steady
and efficient as ever. This happened right around the time that
Fabrizio began devoting himself to the creation of Maria
Lettner. As of that moment he underwent a change so sudden
and striking that Mario realized something else had come up
to absorb his friend's attention, cutting him off from every-

thing—from Mario, from Fulvia, from the tremendous immediate success of *The House on Moon Lake*, which had appeared in bookstores at this same time.

The first edition sold out in two triumphant weeks, and meanwhile the paperback edition of Fritz Oberhofer's biography was ready to come out.

Fabrizio was completely taken up with Maria Lettner; her presence filled his apartment like a fragrance, or like a shadow that sidles up stealthily whenever one turns away, and then playfully runs and hides the moment one tries to look at it. He had let himself sink into a sweet state of weariness a bit like an illness, though painless. It was a sensation similar to what one is supposed to feel when losing blood; something seemed to be flowing slowly out of his body, taking with it, along with his strength, the black clots of his suffering.

His impotent rage against the rest of the world seemed far off and futile now. His forlorn sense of exclusion had undergone a fundamental change in that he now wanted nothing more than for empty abysses to surround the island to which he had fled with his ghost.

In the morning he would remain in bed, half-asleep, for long periods of time; he would turn on the radio but would not listen to it; he did all his shopping by telephone, having his order delivered to the apartment; he ate little and irregularly, either in bed or in front of the television; he watched all the programs with equal indifference, from endless tennis matches to evening game shows.

He went out only when exhorted by Mario to take part in the receptions, encounters and debates he had organized as promotion for *The House on Moon Lake*. He would show up looking much thinner than usual, his pale face etched with sickly shadows, as though he had brought only part of himself—a dry, empty skin such as snakes leave between rocks in springtime after their annual sloughing.

Fulvia also attended these functions.

"Are you sure you're all right?" she would ask him.

"Oh, yes, quite all right," the snakeskin would respond, then he would slip away at the first opportunity.

"If you ask me, there's something wrong with him; I think he's ill," she said later to Mario.

"Nonsense," he said. "It's a perfectly normal reaction. First the big hopes, then the hard work and now the big success. For months he's kept going on nerves alone; now it's as though he's turned off all the lights inside him. It's a way to rest, a mechanism that is activated automatically. The human body knows how to take care of itself, at least most of the time."

They led him around to bookstores all over Italy like a ghost on a leash. During a lecture that he gave at the Austrian Cultural Institute in Rome, he stared the whole time into the space before him, as though not seeing any of those who were listening to him. When it was over, he slipped away amid the applause like someone running off to rejoin his soul. Even Mario could see that he was acting strangely but he was truly convinced that it was a normal reaction and he repeated to Fulvia: "Don't worry, the human body can take care of itself."

"That I don't doubt, I assure you," she said. "But he's so changed . . . I hope he's all right."

Fabrizio, during his first few days of listlessness, had lazily toyed with the idea that he might be ill—low blood pressure perhaps, or else a state of general exhaustion due to overwork. On a couple of occasions—on a Sunday or in the middle of the night—it occurred to him that perhaps he should see a doctor. But as soon as a more opportune moment arrived he would forget and do nothing more about it.

When it first came out, the biography of Fritz Oberhofer seemed to follow on the novel's success for a while but then it suddenly took off on its own. Many saw the writer's life as an act of religious obedience, a prophecy fulfilled by the great work of art and the great romance that destiny had held in store for him.

FRITZ OBERHOFER'S LAST THREE YEARS read the headline of the first review to appear, and from then on everyone's attention became more and more centered on the period in which the writer lived in Mondsee, especially around the figure of Maria Lettner.

The story of the two lovers' relationship gave new life to all the talk about love that had already been in vogue for several years. In the fall *Das Haus am Mondsee* and the biography of Fritz Oberhofer came out in Germany, and were soon to be published in many other countries as well. Newspapers all over the world began to talk about the two books.

Again the interest in the biography—and particularly in Fritz Oberhofer's last mistress—seemed to pass the novel by and leave it behind. Of course, the conviction that one of the more sublime narrative works of the twentieth century had been discovered remained unchanged; but the story of Fritz and Maria transcended the purely literary event; it became fashionable, creating a wave of popularity for the female protagonist so that she soon became a myth.

Mario was besieged by directors wanting to buy the film rights to Fritz Oberhofer's biography; the bidding war was finally won by a German who intended to focus his film entirely on the figure of Maria Lettner. Fashion designers soon launched the Maria Lettner look, which all the women's magazines then presented from every possible angle.

In Italy's most prestigious weekly, the country's most venerable and popular psychologist published a "Love Letter to Maria Lettner."

Mario had thought the biography quite good and had published it gladly, but he had never dreamed it would create such a sensation.

He decided to reread the preface that he had rejected just to see if he hadn't made the mistake of underestimating

Fabrizio's work, but his initial conviction emerged reinforced from a second reading. It was irritating, off-putting, he thought. But once again he stopped there, unable to say precisely where it went wrong, merely that it oozed smugness and false modesty like someone engaged in self-promotion.

Thus, while his friend was drifting further and further into a fatal delirium—identifying with a dead man in order to live out a love story with a woman who had never existed—he, who had in his hand the key to it all, thought nothing of it, and did nothing to help him.

Fabrizio no longer even bothered to cross the street to go read the reviews.

"Have copies made for me and leave them with the doorman," he said to Mario. "And ask them to send everything they have on Fritz Oberhofer and Maria Lettner. Did you know that the newspapers now talk about them without even mentioning the name of the publishing house?"

"So what? Just worry about what concerns you and your work. If they don't mention us anymore, what's it to you?"

"Actually, it means a lot to me. Look, don't be such a stiff. I helped you make a ton of money," retorted Fabrizio, with a hint in his tone of their old manner of conversing.

It was true that Mario—or actually both of them—had made a lot of money on the novel and the biography. What's more, no one had been able to find an original copy of *Das Haus am Mondsee*. Thus, although the book was in the public domain, all the interested foreign publishers had had to work from the photocopies that Fabrizio had made after finally managing to get his hands on the book for a few hours. It was a very unusual legal situation; Mario was quite gentlemanly with his foreign colleagues, though not altogether disinterested.

Fabrizio spent hours on end with his clippings, reading and rereading them, filing them away. The approaching winter

seemed colder and wetter than ever before. This was yet
another reason not to leave his apartment; he couldn't bear
the feeling of the cold air working its way inside his sleeves.
The wet streets seemed to inch up gray and dirty through the
bottoms of his shoes, to the soles of his feet, past the ankles
and up, up, contaminating him until they numbed his very
soul.

In early November a German weekly published a photo
feature on the places where Fritz and Maria had lived and
loved together, images much like those already presented on
many occasions by other periodicals: the lake, the guesthouse,
the room in which the two had slept. What was different about
this piece was that it contained an interview with an elderly
woman who had known Maria as a child, before she met Fritz.

Fabrizio had expected something like this to happen, but
at the time he had not worried much about it. Now that his
expectation had come true, however, he felt a growing sense
of alarm. He had ended the biography with Fritz's death,
saying nothing of what had been the fate of his mistress. He
now regretted not having made her die in 1914 or 1915, to
preclude the possibility of unknown witnesses coming out
with incongruous details that would mar his portrait. The
woman who claimed to have been a childhood companion of
Maria's must have been, of necessity, at least ninety years old;
hence one could reasonably entertain doubts as to the freshness of her memory or that of anyone else of the same age, for
that matter. Moreover, her recollections reconfirmed Maria
Lettner's personality point by point, without altering or dis-
torting it in any way. In the end Fabrizio actually felt pleased
with the interview and thankful toward the little old woman
for having presented such nice, correct memories of Maria's
early years.

Hence it was not the interview in itself that disturbed him.
But if someone in his sixties, or more than one, were, in some
indiscreet, crass and yet not altogether dismissible manner

(arteriosclerotic unreliability no longer being an issue), to come out and claim—taking advantage of the fact that the date of Maria's death had never been established—to have known her around the time, say, when she was forty, when they were already grown up enough to preserve clear memories of things and she still young enough to be considered fully responsible for her own image, and if they began telling unacceptable or conflicting stories about that period, stories which, in short, beclouded and in the end—God forbid—destroyed the figure of Maria Lettner . . . Well, if that were to happen, he would have only his lack of foresight to blame.

Good God, all he would have had to do was to say that Maria herself had died less than a year after Fritz's death . . . and although one always tries, when writing, to avoid melodrama at all costs, there is no denying that death, in the end, is an utterly commonplace occurrence and that mortality, even in the most advanced countries, is always for keeps. It would have sufficed to say that in 1914, for whatever reason, Maria had died, and everything would have been in order. How many people could have possibly threatened her image with a reliable testimony dating back to before 1914? Yes, there were grammar-school memories and that sort of thing, but who would have bothered? He knew damn well that the world was full of imbeciles who always had to say their two cents' worth about everything, full of mythomaniacs, madmen—why then had he not eliminated, from the start, every chance they might have had to make trouble?

The fact was that Fabrizio had not expected any of the ballyhoo that had erupted around the figure of Maria Lettner. He had, of course, hoped the biography of Fritz Oberhofer would meet with modest success, even tremendous success, foreign translations and all; but he had no idea that Maria could ever be, so to speak, extrapolated from the book to such a degree that she would take wing toward her own personal success. He thought he could keep her for himself alone—not closed between the covers of the book in which she was born, but free to flutter about, to fill his house with her presence, to call to him in very faint whispers, to wave to him through half-open doors, to embrace him at night in the dark.

All these things that were happening to Maria beyond the walls of his home were alarming. It was too much. He had no explanation for the sudden flowering of additional details around her person; he didn't bother to think of any. Such things as explanations belonged to a faraway world governed by rigid conventions of logic and covered as it were by a graph of artificial coordinates along which people moved about, crossing paths and coming together in fits and starts, stiff as mechanized puppets. Space and time, as they existed in the world outside, were of no interest to him; but within the walls of his apartment they were sinuous, meandering things, as fluid and resilient as a honeysuckle branch down which he and Maria could glissade together in harmonious, spiral movements.

Hence it did not matter to him *why* certain things happened; it was the fact that they happened at all that alarmed him. Now when he waited for the clippings that Mario sent up to him from time to time, his usual eagerness was mixed with a feeling of great danger.

In late November a French magazine published a long feature on the film about Maria Lettner that the German director had just finished shooting. A few stills of the leading actress were presented alongside a number of portraits of Maria.

There was a striking resemblance between the character and the actress. Moreover, the old photographs, much to Fabrizio's relief, did not conflict with the physiognomy he had given his creation. The face was right, as were the carriage of the head and the slender waist.

Fabrizio had nothing against others' adding details to Maria's portrait; he was far from being jealous, as long as every new contribution served to corroborate the qualities he himself had given her. Only a change in Maria's character brought about through outside intervention could take her away from him. She filled up his life precisely because she was the way she was—with those eyes, that disposition, that walk —and because he had conceived her that way. Theirs was a perfect, closed circle in which Fabrizio was creator and worshiper, Maria creature and goddess. The sudden rush of other believers to the shrine did not bother him; actually, it rather flattered him, as long as they worshiped his goddess without corrupting his creature.

Then other things came out—other articles appeared, accompanied by documentation, photographs, letters and testimony of every sort—and with each passing day Fabrizio's fear proved more and more groundless. Nothing of what was added to Maria's portrait had even so much as a comma out of place. Every detail seemed to have been extracted from the submerged part of the iceberg that corresponds to all those things an author knows about a character but neglects to mention in order to leave room for the other people in his story.

Yet while these developments were dispelling Fabrizio's initial fear, an undefinable malaise began slowly to take hold of him, rising up like a shadow behind him, sinister and menacing, whenever he had his mind on something else, then vanishing into the darkness like a wild animal as soon as he turned to see what it was.

Fabrizio found himself snapping out of his reveries more and more often as though a strange, incomprehensible and yet urgent warning signal were trying to incite him to act, to take hold of himself, to protect himself against some unspeakable horror looming before him.

After having so dreaded the distortion of Maria's image, now, on the contrary, he felt threatened by this very accumulation of elements so perfectly consistent with the character as he had conceived her.

He remained for several days like a frightened animal,

waiting around for the clippings that Mario sent up to him, keeping his mental and physical activity to a bare minimum, lying in bed for hours at a time, slow and cautious as he opened doors and passed from one room to the next as though surrounded by objects delicately poised and ready to come crashing down at the slightest jolt.

ONE DAY HE REALIZED what was happening; Maria existed without him. Maria—*his* Maria that is, not some hack journalist's counterfeit—had acquired a far more substantial existence than the one he had given her; she was now alive and independent of him. She roamed alone through the world he despised, the world of meridians and parallels, the world where testimonies and documents serve not as truth's humble supports but as its substitutes. The few pages he had written had shrunk, becoming no more than an outline, a suggestion; after which she seemed to have emerged by herself, seizing in earnest the life he had given her only in make-believe, going her own way, leaving him behind. The problem was one of degree; the same corroborations of her character that at first had made him feel somewhat flattered to think that Maria could be loved by so many for the very qualities that he had given her, now had the effect of taking her away, of making her autonomous, of breaking the magic circle. It was an act of rebellion, of unspeakable impudence; the creature was defying her creator.

She had stepped out of fiction and gone back to those days on the Mondsee at the start of the century to scatter traces everywhere, offering herself freely to anyone who wanted to look for her, leaving behind photographs, letters, locks of hair and God knows what else.

She had set the Others in motion, legitimizing them, collaborating with them, helping them to take the words out of his mouth, to appropriate what was his the way they always did, driving him into a corner with their chatter—the lies, impostures, trivialities and tricks. What mattered was not the quality and nature of their words—it was the quantity that counted, the never-ending torrent.

His mind now groped about aimlessly in search of an explanation for this sudden plethora of documents relating to Maria Lettner. He thought of many, but all of them seemed equally useless, incapable of canceling each other out so that only one remained, incapable even of combining into an acceptable composite. Yet all of them, each by a different route of listless logic, brought him to the same point: a gloomy, painful resentment of Maria Lettner.

He contemplated destroying her, killing her. He wrote out a detailed account of the research he had conducted in Austria, telling how and why he had come to invent the last three years of Fritz Oberhofer's life, Maria included. The tone, in appearance, was one of confession; yet perfectly legible between the lines was a sense of satisfaction at having taken the whole world for a ride.

While writing he took pleasure in the thought that he was about to bring on Maria's ruin and emerge triumphant, exposing all the petty cheats, imbeciles and pretenders who had fallen into his trap.

When he had finished and was about to leave the house with the manuscript tucked under his arm, a moment of indecision held him back, a fraction of a second that was to drive him ever deeper into the labyrinth that he had entered and leave its mark forever on literary history.

Wondering what newspaper he ought to take his manuscript

to, he stopped in the doorway, then stepped back inside and closed the door.

The telephone rang and at once his heart filled with the unrealistic hope that it was Fulvia; she was his love, his salvation, and yet a morbid cowardice had made him run away from her. He shouted her name as he ran toward the receiver with hands outstretched.

There was no one on the line. The phone had not rung more than three or four times; whoever was calling had given up quickly. He tried calling the office himself; Mario responded with surprise, as a long time had passed since Fabrizio had asked for Fulvia.

"You want to speak to Fulvia?" he asked as though unsure he had heard right.

"Yes, yes, put her on!"

"But Fabrizio, it's past eight! She left quite a while ago."

He tried her house, but got no answer. He called Mario again.

"Are you sure she's in Milan? Might she have gone to Valtellina?"

"Not a chance. She has to come in to work tomorrow just like any other day."

"Well, she's not at home."

"She must have gone out to eat."

"Out to eat?"

"What's with you, Fabrizio?"

"Out to eat?" he repeated, stunned.

"Yessir. Let me quote you something, it's from the Song of Songs: 'Tell me, o thou whom my soul loveth, where thou feedest thy flock, for why should I be as one who turneth aside by the flocks of thy companions?' "

"What?"

"Have you been drinking?"

"No. I'm going to try calling her again. Good-bye."

He dialed Fulvia's number again. By now he felt as though

he could not make any decisions without first talking to her. There was no answer; surely she must have gone out to eat.

He collapsed into an armchair, totally perplexed and unable to think. He would try Fulvia again in a half hour. In the meantime he started to reread his manuscript. When he reached the last line a huge sinister burst of laughter erupted from a dark corner of the house, echoed in every room and bounded on top of him with the force of a tropical storm, reducing him to a pitiful lump of rags.

Who, today, would ever believe such things?

Even to his own eyes it all seemed like rubbish, a pathetic attempt at self-promotion or else the raving of a sick mind. He remained motionless for a long time, annihilated. From time to time he would reread a bit, now and then redialing Fulvia's number, the intervals growing longer and longer and each time more swollen with apathy until—the whole night having passed in this manner and a white winter's dawn now rising—he admitted defeat. To speak to Mario, the principal victim of his fraud, would have been absurd. He was beyond help.

He gathered all his clippings, reviews, articles and photos, and put them in a large envelope together with his text. He sealed it, then wrote on it: "Keep this concealed and open it only if something should happen to me." He put this in a second envelope, went down to the post office, which was opening just then, and mailed it to Fulvia. He himself did not know what he had in mind, aside from a vague desire, before his surrender, to make things "normal" again.

He was awakened around noon by the telephone; there was a woman at the other end, speaking in German.

"Mr. Fabrizio Garrone? Excuse me, I don't speak Italian, but you of course speak my language, do you not?"

"Yes, of course. What can I do for you?"

"You don't know me . . . I had wanted to write you, but then I thought it better to talk to you directly. My name is Petra Ebner."

"Ah . . . Delighted to know you. Where are you calling from?"

"I'm in Mondsee, at home. I wanted to tell you that I have read your excellent biography of Fritz Oberhofer, and I send my compliments . . ."

"Why, thank you, you're very kind."

"But that's not the only reason I called. I wanted to inform you that I have, in my possession, a number of letters written by Fritz Oberhofer to Maria Lettner. You see, Herr Garrone, Maria Lettner was my grandmother."

"*Your grandmother?*"

"Yes, that's right, my grandmother. And these letters are very beautiful . . . I think they are worth publishing, and I think you would be the right person to see to this . . ." She broke off, then began again with a bit of hesitation in her voice: "You *are* interested, aren't you? You're not too busy, I hope?"

"I . . . no, no, I'm not busy at all . . . You have letters from Fritz Oberhofer to Maria Lettner?"

"Precisely. If you think you'd be interested . . . You see, I wouldn't want to send them by mail, and I really don't think I could come to Milan. I . . . I'm afraid I'm not much of a traveler. But if you wanted to come to Austria I would be more than happy to put you up and help you in every way possible."

"My good Frau Ebner . . . or is it Fräulein Ebner?"

"Fräulein."

"My good Fräulein Ebner, all this comes as something of a surprise to me."

"I imagined it would."

Was it just his impression, or was her tone sharp, sarcastic, if not downright menacing? Was it possible—and here his heart filled with hope—was it possible that this woman had proof of his forgery and wanted to blackmail him? Was it possible that he had found an unwitting ally in his plan to destroy Maria Lettner?

The postmark on the envelope he sent to Fulvia would prove that he had intended to expose his fraud before receiving Petra Ebner's telephone call, provided it was possible to trace an international call and establish at what time of day it had been made. Was it possible? It had to be, he thought, and he felt glad he had the foresight to send off the envelope.

Not that it really made much difference; his main concern was driving Maria back into the world of shadows where she belonged. So much the better—though it was not absolutely necessary—if his intention to reveal the truth appeared to be voluntary rather than extorted by blackmail.

What he had to do now was to make this woman think that he was afraid of what she knew, to act as though he was ready to do anything just to keep her from talking . . . The more convinced she was of his fear, the bolder she would become, and the sooner she would show her hand and come out with her threat—which to Fabrizio would not be a threat but a sweet, sweet promise. How would a frightened person act in this situation? He probably would rush off to talk to her face to face, to try to negotiate. . . .

"I really hadn't expected anything like this, but as you can well imagine, I am very interested. It is indeed a surprise, but a wonderful surprise."

"So you will come?"

"Yes, of course. If I can get a reservation I'll come right away, on tomorrow's flight. Unfortunately there are no direct flights to Salzburg. I'll have to go by way of Zurich, but I should be in Mondsee by four in the afternoon. If there's a snag, I'll let you know."

He took down her address, thanked her for calling and hung up.

Perhaps there was still hope for him. If only there was some way to affix a postmark, a seal of authenticity to this hope as well. At that moment, the foggy vagueness, the blur in which he had been seeking refuge all his life, seemed like a hostile element he could no longer control, overwhelmed as he was by forces far more proficient than he at moving among all the elusive spirals and undulating underwater stalks and stems.

He rolled a sheet of paper into the typewriter and wrote:

Dear Fulvia, If I could ever explain to you why the world—or perhaps just the age I live in—seems so alien to me, you would understand why, even while wanting precisely the opposite, I have done everything I can to lose you, fleeing from you as I flee from everything else. But unfortunately I don't know the reason. I know that the blame does not lie entirely with the rubbish strewn across the countryside, the obscene world of politics and the parlor games that have in most cases taken the place of culture; I am also to blame, and it is this guilt that I am unable to analyze, whereas I could go on for a thousand pages listing the world's monstrosities, and you would have to agree with me on every point. So let's leave it at this—that I know I, too, am in the wrong.

You are already familiar with the mess I've gotten myself into, since if you are reading this letter, you will have already opened the envelope I sent to you this morning. To this mess another element has now been added, and it may represent either a further complication or the ultimate solution. A few minutes ago I received a telephone call from a certain Petra Ebner, Apfelbaumstrasse 13, Mondsee, who claims to be Maria Lettner's granddaughter and to possess letters written by Fritz Oberhofer to her grandmother. I am leaving tomorrow to try to get to the bottom of this. All my love, Fabrizio.

He sealed the envelope and wrote on it: "Read this too, if you decide to open the packet I sent to you this morning." He put it in another envelope and raced back to the post office to send it to Fulvia's address as well.

131

Part III

PETRA

AFTER THE TAXI HAD GONE, Fabrizio stood alone in front of the house without moving, lost in unconscious contemplation. When he finally came around and rang the bell on the small gate of black wood, the scene was deeply impressed on his mind, as though the place had always existed in his memory, its placid, austere charm winning him over without surprise, like an old, familiar feeling.

Upon arriving at the lake he was pleased to find the same landscape that had greeted his eyes on his first visit there. Gone were the miniature golf courses and the swimming pools; the summer trappings, together with the tourists, had been swept away by the December gloom. The mountaintops formed a circle of white all around the disk of blue sky suspended over the valley, which had returned to its original orderly state.

Petra Ebner's house was right on the lake, a little bit outside the town. It was two stories high and plastered white. The roof and the balcony running along two sides of the house were made of dark wood. The yard was shielded from the road by a row of black fir trees and contained, in the part exposed to the sun, a small, well-tended orchard, about twenty trees in all—apple trees, he thought—which were bare and leafless at this time of year.

The house presented the same picture of neatness as the rest of the town. What made it different and unique was its aura of monastic renunciation of all frivolity. It was more noble than graceful, more peacefully harmonious than welcoming.

Yet none of these qualities seemed attributable to objective elements alone—such as the relationships between the building's height and width, the gentle sloping of the lawn toward the lake, the colors (or rather, their absence) or the signs of diligent, daily maintenance. All were undeniably there but there was something else as well. The house's subtler, indescribable aspects seemed to cast a spell. Fabrizio did not know whether to consider it a *good* or an *evil* spell; clearly he had been struck by something old and familiar, something perhaps from a childhood fairy tale. But he could not tell whether the house that he seemed to recognize belonged to a fairy or a witch.

The woman who appeared at the entrance was white and black, just like her house.

Her face was pale, as were the hands that emerged from the long sleeves of her dress, which was black as the long, straight hair gathered on her head. Her clothes, bearing and hairstyle tended to discourage anyone who might see her from wondering whether she was young or pretty. Her entire attitude almost forced one to dismiss evaluations of this sort as improper. She herself had eliminated the question from consideration. And since she radiated the same austere, placid authority that Fabrizio had felt emanating from the house, her resolve imposed itself on anyone who looked at her, disallowing an entire category of criteria.

For this same reason one could neither describe her as old or ugly. Fabrizio could only come up with a short list of objective traits: tall, quite thin, probably somewhere between thirty and forty years of age, with black hair and eyes.

She walked toward him along the little footpath, her steps harmonious and absolutely neuter; the gait of a priest, thought Fabrizio, or the flight of a seagull, the peaceful flowing of a river . . .

Inside, the house was not much of a surprise, as it was noble, severe and not very welcoming, just as he had expected. The feeling persisted that this place belonged to a region buried deep in his memory, where all things seen or imagined in childhood live on. If it was not in a fairy tale, it might have been in the Holy Scriptures; or perhaps it was the house of Socrates or the monastery at Casamari where his great-uncle was abbot, a building he had seen only once—when he and Teodora had gone there to take their First Communion—but had never forgotten.

He was not even sure if the thing that this house reminded him of was actually another house; it might have been a thought, a person, a dream.

What he thought he was seeing was that here, in this place, the point, the line, the plane and space itself—concepts which, having zero and infinity as their only possible measures, defy all material representation and actually lie beyond the grasp of the human mind, except in awkward approximations—reigned in their purest, most essential forms.

And like the definition of point, line or plane, his first words were inadequate. He said: "This place is extraordinary. So peaceful, harmonious."

"Do you like it?" Even Petra Ebner's voice was like her house. "You know," she continued, "as I told you on the phone, I think your biography of Fritz Oberhofer is brilliant . . . a very fine piece of work . . ."

"Thank you."

". . . very fine, though I must say it contains a few minor inaccuracies."

Here we go, thought Fabrizio. She hasn't even given me the time to sit down and she's already come to the point. So much the better. He had brought a suitcase with enough clothes for a three-or-four-day stay, expecting long, drawn-out negotiations.

"Really?" he said. "I would be very grateful if you could point out my mistakes."

On the plane he had considered the possibility that Petra Ebner might have no intention whatsoever of blackmailing him but hoped instead to make a few waves herself by taking advantage of the fact that she had a grandmother named Maria Lettner. After all, he had given the character a last name typical of the region and a very common first name precisely because it made him feel he was working on more solid ground, since there must have been at least *one* Maria Lettner actually living during that period. If this was the case, that is, if Petra Ebner was just a silly fool who wanted to see her name in the papers, he would merely come away having made a useless trip with nothing gained and nothing lost.

And if this was not the case? Well, if this Petra really did have proof that Maria Lettner was an invention, he wanted that proof. What did it matter if he wanted it just to make it public, and not to suppress it, as this woman believed?

Thus he had decided to act as naturally as possible, without adopting an *als ob* strategy, for he was convinced that his and Petra's respective positions in this game were already, in essence, perfectly *as if*.

He wanted her proof and he wanted to pay as little as possible for it. His plan therefore was to show a reasonable amount of interest in the matter, just enough to make her feel confident of securing a decent sum from him, but to make her understand as well that there were limits to what he could pay, and that if her demands became excessive he would lose interest in the whole thing and make no deal at all.

"You know," he said, "I could, eventually, do a revised and corrected edition, in which case your advice would be very valuable."

But the woman no longer seemed in any hurry to settle the matter.

"Oh, they're just little things," she said. "Come see the view of the lake from this window."

"Extraordinary."

For the rest of the evening she did not say another word about the inaccuracies in Fabrizio's book, or even about Fritz's letters to Maria, the pretext for their meeting. Petra's conversation unfolded at a quiet, geometric pace; it did not seem like fertile ground for fantasy or lies. Fabrizio felt certain that the account she was giving him of Maria Lettner's life was not made up. She was probably relating the experiences of her grandmother exactly as she remembered them; the only falsehood lay in her ascribing them to an imaginary person.

"This is one of the oldest houses in town," she told him. "It was my grandmother's idea to have the balcony built upstairs, after she married Grandfather in 1914; the rest, I believe, is exactly how it was when the house was first built a long time ago."

"It gives one a feeling of infinite peace," said Fabrizio.

He had already moved into his room, which was on the second floor. It was large and square with wooden floorboards. He had lingered there alone for a while, putting his things away in the drawers, looking around, gazing out onto the lake.

Along one wall, between two tall bookcases that reached as high as the ceiling, was a large double bed with white covers. In front of it, on both sides of the window, stood two built-in closets, which extended the recess in the wall, creating a cubicle that contained, perpendicular to the plane of the outside wall, a small inclined writing table and a built-in bench covered with a canvas cushion.

This little nook reminded him of the *Saint Jerome in His Study* that had accompanied him through thick and thin and was now waiting for him back in Milan. He had always believed that with a niche such as this at his disposal—so

139

quiet, secluded and yet open to the outside world—he could conceive great thoughts, write sublime works. Both the house in which he was born and lived until he completed his studies and his apartment in Milan had walls thick enough to allow the construction of a cubicle that would have fulfilled his desire; apparently, though, this desire had never been strong enough to induce him to undertake the task of moving one of the radiators that occupied the spaces beneath all the windows in his apartment. Or else—as was the case with most of his desires—it was strong but not vital, like a galvanic spasm.

And so he had kept on dreaming of a universal focal point of this sort, a perfectly sheltered spot from which, tucked away as in a shell, he might master all human knowledge as contained in the books there gathered and still have all around him the sky, the stars and the open air like an endless road leading everywhere at once.

Now as they dined in the living room at a rectangular table covered with a white cloth and illuminated by a chandelier of burnished brass, Petra talked to him of Maria Lettner.

"Grandmother was over thirty when she met Grandfather. You see, she enjoyed a decent private income—she owned a sawmill on the other side of the lake, as well as the woods below Drachenstein."

"But she was also a beautiful, fascinating woman. You're not trying to say that your grandfather only married her for the estate that she brought as her dowry?"

"Oh, I don't know. He was very stern and old-fashioned. He was Protestant—money and virtue, in his ethical geography, did not stand in the same sort of relation to each other as they do for us Catholics. He never asked Grandmother about her past, though he certainly must have heard some of the talk. I'm sure that for him, an attractive thirty-three-year-old woman—single, independent and the object of gossip—would hardly have been acceptable without an estate. Whereas, surrounded as she was by the authority of wealth, he quite naturally—disinterestedly, I mean—came to see her as belonging to another category; she became an interesting woman, modern, emancipated . . . But then I really don't know; in my earliest memories of him he was already over eighty years old."

"Perhaps, on the other hand, he fell madly in love with her precisely because she seemed so unsuitable."

"Who knows. He was a doctor, from Linz. He had come here to recuperate from an illness, something with the lungs, I think; in those days there didn't seem to be any other kind of illness. Later, when he married Grandmother, he moved his practice to Mondsee. Their first child, a boy, died in infancy; a few years later my mother was born. She remained an only child—an only daughter I should say. We're a line of only daughters—my grandmother, my mother and I. My mother and father married at the start of the war; he was an officer in the Wehrmacht and died at Cassino. I never knew him."

"So your grandfather was the head of the household when you were a child?"

Could this explain the naked, crystalline, mystical transparence that reigned in that house? Even if that stern moralist—after permitting his wife to have the balcony built—had not in fact made any other changes in the structure of the house, he still could have left his imprint through a long series of slight modifications, all of the same nature. Removing something here, refusing to replace something there, leveling, neutralizing. He must have left his mark on this house—and much more profoundly than if he had moved a wall or added a room. And he must have left his mark on little Petra as well, judging from the results.

And where did Maria figure in all this? Did she count for nothing? Had she traded in her willful disposition, her imagination, her joy, for a proper, normal marriage? Had it been a painful renunciation or a delicious submission to a mortal peace that she had wanted to enjoy while her senses were

still alive, though a bit numbed—like flaccid tentacles sway-
ing in slow, lazy waves, immersed in a soft, tepid element?

"Yes, he ran all of our lives."

"And how did your grandmother feel about living under
the rule of this stern, old-fashioned man, as you called him?"
No sooner had he asked this question than he realized he had
once again let himself get carried away into taking the existence of Maria Lettner seriously. He had imagined a melancholy
Maria caught in a confining, boring marriage, and, forgetting
that she did not exist, that she had to be driven back into
nonexistence and that this was the very reason he had
come here, he had fallen right into the trap, had let his indig-
nation get the better of him, like someone who had suffered a
betrayal, a betrayal perpetrated for base, shameful reasons;
how wretched that respectability, how shabby that security.

"Grandmother lived on for several years after Grandfather's
death; my memories of her are from that period, not from
before then. She was usually the one who took care of me,
since my mother worked—ran the sawmill, that is. Grandmother and I sometimes went fishing together . . . She would
tell me wonderful stories, and she taught me the names of
flowers and birds. She was so fanciful, a real daydreamer . . .
You never knew whether she was talking in earnest or just
joking, whether she made things up or was just confused. She
would play the piano, especially in winter, because it was good
for her circulation, she said. She once told me about an
amazing cake that they eat in England, called carpet cake,
which is made with a throw rug washed seven times and then
filled with dried prunes . . . Once, when we went mushroom
picking together, she found a family of nineteen porcini mushrooms in a hollow, all of them identical and hard as rocks. She
left me there to watch over them as she went to look for a
farmer to witness her discovery; she did this, she said, because
no one would ever have believed either one of us when we told
them that all those little marvels had grown together simul-

taneously in that small corner of the woods barely one meter square in size. She was right, of course, because no one ever did believe what she said, and I was just a child."

"She must have been a fantastic grandmother."

"Oh, yes. But my dear mother was very good to me too. She died four years ago."

"And since then you've lived alone?"

"Yes, but life is never empty for those who have religion. Some people think that going to mass every morning is enough, but fighting the Evil One is hard work, and one's work is never done. Of course, we all have to practice our faith, but we also have to struggle, to keep a constant watch . . . There are the parish gatherings, the committees . . . I also have the sawmill to take care of, and I like to read, to embroider . . . and then with Salzburg so close by, there's always good music to hear."

"And what did your grandmother play on the piano?"

"A bit of everything. Schubert, 'Die Tiroler sind lustig, Es geht alles vorüber' . . . Even tavern songs, like 'Fein, fein schmeckt uns der Wein' . . ."

Petra pronounced the names of songs in the same tone in which she had recounted the little whimsies that had been Maria's way of linking her last years with her joyous past, of getting through and beyond her long days of penance. The words came out like limpid drops of emotionless sound, following one another in perfect order, never colliding, never clouding, never echoing unduly.

When, in the days that followed, Fabrizio thought back on this and other conversations with Petra, he could not understand why they left him with such a strong feeling of sublime symmetry; it seemed the only explanation was that the words she had spoken were other than he remembered them, that once they had made their indelible mark in his consciousness, they had been destroyed, like a secret message, leaving no compromising traces behind.

Whatever the case, what remained most deeply impressed on his mind from that evening were the coordinates of that portrait, the necessary points that determined the figure's contours. Yet the real Maria Lettner, with her songs and fantasies, seemed incompatible with the voice that had told of it all, just as she had seemed incompatible with the room in which those words had echoed.

Fabrizio thought that the house must have undergone other, slow transformations after Maria's death, being gradually purged with each passing year—first by Petra's mother, the nameless widow, then by Petra herself—purged of every earthly, fleshly element. And yet preserving, perhaps, something of Maria's spirit, since the house, as he saw it at that moment, was no more the house of the doctor from Linz, the old-fashioned zealot, than it was the house of the warm, sweet, ingenious, whimsical Maria.

Perhaps there was a third presence, different from these two, that had culled the subtler essences of the sternness and beauty of the other two, fusing them into sober geometries and filling the space with that pure air cleansed of sin and pain. He wondered whether Petra had done it all herself in the last four years, or whether the real author of this whole scene, Petra included, might not in fact be her mother, the vertex of the first family triangle—the doctor, Maria, herself—and later the central link in the chain of women—Maria, herself, Petra.

He did not inquire about this person, because she seemed to him to represent the unfathomable zero factor of the formula that concealed, like a coded message, the family secret.

Soon it was bedtime and Petra brought Fabrizio a small tray with a glass and a bottle of cognac.

"The ladies must retire now," she said. "If you would like a book to read, I'm sure you can find something of interest in the small library in your room."

She started toward the stairs like a figure from another age.

As Fabrizio's room had its own private bathroom, her decision to go upstairs before him seemed not to correspond to any practical necessity but to some ancient rule of etiquette. It seemed as though Petra's knowledge of certain things in life came only from the nineteenth-century novels that lined the shelves upstairs. No doubt she drove her car along the highway just like everyone else when she had to go to Salzburg, bought her concert ticket like everyone else and did her shopping in town in the most normal of fashions. In certain respects she must have had to keep up with the changes in the outside world. Yet she seemed to have remained untouched by the deeper currents of time's flow, where it affected such intimate matters as personal relationships, friendship and love. She did not even seem to have any direct experience of so common a thing as having a guest in one's house. She was quite calm and self-possessed in her ways, and impeccably polite, but in a manner that harked back to a time fifty, even one hundred years before her birth.

Trying to imagine what kind of life this woman could have had, Fabrizio felt convinced that Petra had enjoyed a short-lived season of natural flowering, taking advantage of a combination of circumstances which, for mysterious reasons, were necessary for her to assume earthly substance and to enter into contact with that slight, disturbing element of mutability that lies within the solidity of objects. It had been necessary for Maria to remain on earth for a while, just as it had been necessary for the doctor from Linz to have left her for his gloomy paradise; with the aid of their respective presence and absence, Petra had been able to go looking for mushrooms, pick flowers and sing tavern songs for a short time, perhaps eight or ten years.

Now the woman was climbing the stairs; she was halfway up, part of her already swallowed up in the darkness of the second floor. All he could see now was the black skirt, the flesh-tone stockings, the nunnish, low-heeled shoes. Suddenly the shoes interrupted their alernating, upward climb and came to rest together on the same stair. Then came the voice from an invisible point above, loud, clear and emphatic:

"*This* is the house. Take a good look, when you go up to bed, at the writing table in your room."

Then the shoes resumed their climb and disappeared.

The words rolled down the stairs and came to a halt at Fabrizio's feet, as he stood alone in the living room below. It was up to him to decide whether to pick them up or leave them there. Every option was open to him, except that of following Petra upstairs and asking her at once for an explanation. The very fact that she had let her declaration drop in that incomplete form, that she had not said—if this was indeed what she had meant—"This is the house where Fritz and Maria lived," proved that she wanted to leave it up to him to decide whether or not to open up a new range of considerations by changing this detail at the beginning of the story.

For if it was here in this house that Fritz had loved Maria and written his masterpiece, and not in the guesthouse by the lake or in any other guesthouse, then the place deserved close examination. Nothing, or very little, had been disfigured or consumed by outside forces. Petra was a priestess, and her mother and grandfather—whatever their moral position vis-à-vis Maria's past—must have been so conservative by nature that the stasis they instilled in the house would have been enough to ensure that no sentiments already in the air could ever be driven out by others.

Fritz and Maria's love had been the last passion to breathe within these walls; then virtue had covered everything, bringing it to a standstill, like the ashes at Pompeii. And so? Where did this discovery lead? Nowhere, probably, or else to a closed ring, a magic circle within which one could only swallow one's tail for eternity.

Fabrizio decided to disregard the questions which until that moment had spurred his curiosity: whether or not Fritz Oberhofer's mistress had actually been Petra's grandmother, whether or not her name had been Maria Lettner, whether or not she was exactly as he had portrayed her; who had come before and who after; whether the past had altered the present or vice versa; who had lied, who had divined the truth. These seemed like minor quibbles that had no bearing on the real mystery, the mystery of the house and the spell it cast over him.

When he entered his room he went to the window at once and sat down at the writing table. He examined the wooden tabletop, naïvely hoping to find a pair of carved initials left there as a kind of message for him.

So the doctor from Linz had not bought the house when he decided to marry Maria and move to Mondsee; he had found it in his bride's trousseau, along with the woods and the sawmill. And along with Fritz's ghost, for this too was part of Maria Lettner's estate, the surest, most incorruptible possession of all, taken on in an inorganic state, immune to all change or surprise.

The woods could catch fire, the sawmill could be confiscated, the house could collapse from a sudden shift in the earth's crust—but nothing and no one could ever threaten Maria's claim to Fritz's ghost. The dour physician from Linz, demiurge of that small geometrical universe, became little more than a paper-doll figure, and his unchallanged rule in that house suddenly seemed to Fabrizio to be an essential part of Maria Lettner's overall design.

With his obtuse rigidity he had made the whole picture static, freezing it forever at the very moment when everything around Maria had settled into the best of possible forms: eternal love, fixed at its moment of greatest splendor by Fritz's death; the respectability and security of married life; and motherhood.

The poor doctor was left with only the illusion of being in command of the household; in reality he had been taken on as a caretaker, to ensure that nothing moved in the picture in which Maria was the central figure.

Fabrizio pursued these and other thoughts as he sat at the

writing table. But no sooner would he get hold of one than it would immediately lose substance, as when one plunges one's hands into the sea to catch the moonlight.

One thing he was sure of, however: if this was indeed the house, then the room that Petra had given him had to be the one in which Fritz and Maria had slept, and the table at which he was seated had to be the writer's worktable.

The house was large, and as there were many other rooms, it might have seemed unlikely that Fritz would have chosen to use only one as both bedroom and study. And yet there was such perfect continuity uniting the rows of books on the shelves at the back of the room, the double bed that they framed, the window cubicle with its sublimely appropriate dimensions and the twofold view, from the worktable, of the lake on the left and the room on the right, that it seemed this had to be the place, the final destination.

Fabrizio remained seated for a long time in that niche, a sweet weariness enveloping him from all sides, like the sensation one is said to feel when freezing to death under a blanket of snow. The silence that surrounded him, neutral and hollow, was endless, spreading out freely in every direction; there seemed not to be a single sound on earth that might stem its flow.

Only much later did Fabrizio go to sleep in Fritz and Maria's bed.

Ever since childhood he had loved the early morning hours. They had always been conducive to action and inspired good common sense in him. Even after a night like the last, the morning's first light still produced a remnant of its former positive effect. It had snowed and the landscape before him appeared newly transformed. After so many months in which everything seemed to change in appearance from one moment to the next for reasons difficult to grasp, he was delighted now to discover a change all around him that was finally attributable to something so obvious as a turn in the weather.

The world seemed like a different place because everything was covered by ten inches of immaculate snow, as anyone could see.

He felt as though a hand were pulling him toward a safe shore, away from deadly illusions. He had to settle his unfinished business with Petra Ebner. She was already back from morning mass. He knew this because he had heard the front door open and close, and because the mild clatter now coming from the kitchen was too subdued and discreet to be produced by the brusque movements of a cleaning woman. Before going downstairs, Fabrizio wanted to reorganize his plans so that he could present himself at the breakfast table with his thoughts in order.

Little by little, the reason for his coming there had drifted away from the center of his consciousness, before finally dissipating altogether at the fringe; putting it back together was no easy task.

Yes, he had to find out whether Petra Ebner had anything to sell him, and if so, to buy it, whatever the price, and return at once to Milan. Why? So that he could make public, as sensationally as possible, the documents and evidence that would destroy Maria Lettner. It was terribly important to him; he had come just for this. How could he ever have forgotten? He had to punish her for having left him all alone while she ran off with the others. Always the Others: architects, magistrates, living-room radicals, snobs, women, students, structuralists, sociologists, columnists—chatterbox crickets of every stripe—blah blah chirp chirp—not to mention the exalted blather of culture's high-heeled foodmongers, purveyors of late-night risottos impressed with the brilliance of their own obviousness—oh, how many times had he thought, "If only I had the right hammer . . . Thwack! That's one. Squashed, spattered on the wall."

And when Maria Lettner had become real, he had desired the same fate for her. How dare you, you ghost.

And yet he knew he was not a bad man. It was just that

something was always upsetting him, frightening him, and since he felt so naked, so unarmed and inept, all he could do was run off into a corner and snarl through his teeth, dark and impotent.

And now he wanted to do away with poor Maria. How vile.

And how absurd. Things, in reality, were much simpler than that. The snow had covered everything, and now the landscape—once brown, green, black—had turned all white. Plain and simple. That was how things were in reality. To go outside he would have to put on heavy shoes. Right.

The biography of Fritz Oberhofer had, for some time now, kept him from the clutches of poverty. Right. Fulvia was a fabulous woman and he—at the bottom of his heart—had enough love for her to make her happy, if he could only be a little less tortuous. And she loved him too, which made him think that he still might be in time to snatch her back by her strawberry-blond hair. Plain and simple as the snow.

He decided to be frank with Petra. If she really did have the letters of Fritz Oberhofer to his last mistress, whatever her name and whatever her relation to Petra, he would see to their publication. He had nothing against adding to his fame and to his bank account. If, on the other hand, he was given to understand that she wanted to blackmail him, he would tell her to do as she pleased and then leave at once.

———— 18 ————

HE CAME DOWN THE STAIRS beaming with confidence. The table was already set.

"Good morning," said Petra. "Your coffee will be ready in just a minute. In the meantime make yourself comfortable."

On the shelf beside the front door, a missal and a pair of gloves lay next to a carefully folded black veil.

Petra and Fabrizio sat down across from one another.

"You haven't yet told me anything about Fritz Oberhofer," he said.

"What could I possibly tell you? You know much more about him than I."

"Yes, but you're the one with the letters. You called me because of those letters, and I have certainly made no secret of that fact that they are of great interest to me."

"Oh, the letters. I'm sure you'll agree that they're very beautiful."

"Don't you want to show them to me?"

"Of course, but you don't think I keep them at home, do you? They're in a safe-deposit box, at the bank." She raised her eyes from her cup and looked at Fabrizio. "And today is Saturday," she added.

"Fräulein Ebner," said Fabrizio, trying to sound very serious, though the words still came out shrill and petulant, "you don't mean to tell me that you invited me to come here all the way from Milan, knowing full well I would arrive Friday afternoon—because I told you—and you didn't take the trouble of withdrawing the letters from the bank! Let's lay our cards on the table. I don't know who your grandmother was, or what her name might have been, and I really don't care. But I can tell you that Maria Lettner never existed, that I invented her myself, which of course you already know. And let me add that none of this is of any importance whatsoever, in case you were hoping to make something out of it. The biography that I wrote has been published all over the world; it has brought me success. I don't think it would make much difference to me if you were to reveal—as I, moreover, was planning to do myself—that I invented Maria. So please give me the letters, tell me how much you want, and let's be done with it."

All the while he spoke Petra did not once take her motionless eyes off him. Now she lowered her eyelids momentarily, as if to reexamine under the cover of their shadow what she had just heard, the better to grasp its significance.

"Excuse me, but I'm afraid I don't understand," she said finally. "I don't understand how your mind works. You want to buy Fritz Oberhofer's letters to my grandmother, and then you say my grandmother never existed. This is very strange, and it is also very strange that you should suddenly become so aggressive, after being received in this house as a friend."

At that moment Petra's pallid face resembled one of Sassetta's saints—the skin stretching tightly across the cheekbones and the bridge of the nose, then sinking into the shadows of the eye sockets and the hollow cheeks. It was a face that seemed to express an endless capacity for suffering, for accepting suffering nobly. Her two hands resting on the tablecloth looked like two forgotten flowers. Fabrizio noticed for the first time how delicately fragile her wrists were and immediately felt like a brute.

"I'm sorry, Fräulein, I didn't mean to attack you. You are truly an angel and this house is definitely paradise."

"It's all right," she said. "Try to calm down and put your thoughts in order. Let's forget whether or not what you said was discourteous; it was certainly contradictory, don't you think?"

"Ah, consistency, concordance, order, geometry! Truth, Fräulein, is not governed by Euclid's laws. Of course in a place like this, where everything rests in sublime equilibrium, and where you, good Fräulein Ebner, do not so much live as hover about, the temptation is strong to believe so; but it is not the case. It's a much more tangled business than that. Everything coexists with its opposite, and any attempt to create order is utterly useless. We may still manage to make our little rearrangements here and there on the surface, but it takes much more than that. It is wiser to resign oneself to disorder; only from disorder can an occasional glimmer emerge, if at all."

He really should not have been talking so much, he said to himself, or letting himself get carried so far away from the subject he had introduced. But she was prodding him, giving him rope.

"Order, disorder, truth! Perhaps we don't use words the same way, Herr Garrone. Perhaps what you call a glimmer I call delirium."

"Call it what you will. I remember something that happened to me once in Milan, some time ago." (Why wouldn't he stop?) "I was crossing Piazza del Duomo diagonally, a blazing sun shining straight into my eyes. A short distance away I saw a man coming toward me. Two thoughts immediately came into my mind—one right after another, like twins—and then placed themselves parallel to each other. I describe them in this fashion because immediately after this episode I analyzed what had taken place in my brain and I distinctly remembered that the two thoughts had seemed present in physical form,

153

one next to the other; I could feel them there, side by side, one on the right and the other on the left.

"One thought said, *Well, if it isn't Bernardo Vaini!*; the other: *I'll go at once and greet him with a big embrace.* After a few more steps each of the two thoughts was simultaneously erased and replaced by another.

"On the right: *I was mistaken, that's not Bernardo Vaini*; on the left: *I really shouldn't embrace him; we haven't seen each other in quite a while and he probably doesn't even remember me.* I took a few more steps and then a third thought rose up in my head and like a large wave made a clean sweep of my mind from one end to the other, filling the whole space for a brief but decisive moment. It said: *How silly of me to be so shy; of course I should embrace him!* And so, brimming with cheer, I rushed up and embraced a total stranger."

Petra kept looking at him from the other side of the table, sitting so still and so directly in front of him that she seemed to be painted onto the back of her chair.

"And so?" she asked.

"Well, nothing really. What I was trying to say is that sometimes, when thinking, when letting oneself think that way, opening the mind to superimpositions, distortions . . . sometimes, you see, one happens to catch a glimmer or two . . ."

"But you didn't catch anything at all that day in Piazza del Duomo. You merely mistook one person for another and then found yourself in an embarrassing situation."

"That's true, but it was that very moment of embarrassment which shook me awake and made it possible to analyze, in an orderly fashion, my disordered thoughts while they were still very fresh. And I became convinced that the glimmers I had caught in the past—small stuff, I assure you, not a single clear idea in the lot—had always come to me when I had let my mind go off like that on its own."

"I suppose it's possible, if you say so. But what about Grandmother? You said she didn't exist, that you invented her. This is my grandmother we're talking about, Mr. Garrone; you can't make such a statement so lightly. This is not a glimmer of truth, this is something that cannot be. Or perhaps you think that I, too, don't exist?"

Was there a hint of irony in Petra's tone? Did she realize how absurd this conversation was? No, it wasn't possible. The words fell from her lips like a procession down a marble staircase; it seemed indeed that they were all to be taken literally, each and every one.

Fabrizio restrained himself, not wanting to offend her, in part because he felt touched by the delicacy of her wrists, in part because he was full of reverence for her priestly severity.

"What I said was nonsense. Someday I'll explain it to you, if you wish. In any case," he added, convinced that he was expressing the ultimate truth on the Maria Lettner question, "it has something to do with the way I wrote the biography, but it has no bearing on actual people or things."

Petra accepted his apology with a solemn moment of silence.

"Did you bring heavy shoes with you?" she said finally.

"I beg your pardon?"

"If you brought heavy shoes we could go for a walk."

"I have a pair that should be all right."

They were not all right and Fabrizio got his feet wet, but he was content just to walk beside Petra in silence. He had decided to wait for the banks to reopen and have a look at Fritz Oberhofer's letters. During their stroll the rhythm of the passing hours had somehow changed, giving way to a placid flow that allayed all impatience and made all delays acceptable. The house was like a sailboat on a smooth, windless sea; since nothing moved, there was no way of perceiving one's own motionlessness . . . He also thought of Sleeping Beauty, who did not move forward in time because the rest of the castle was also asleep.

On Monday morning Fabrizio drifted out of sleep into a state of sluggish torpor that lasted late into the morning.

When he finally went downstairs he found the table already set, and on it a Thermos of coffee and a note: "Good morning! I'll be home at one."

He figured that after morning mass Petra had probably gone to the sawmill and perhaps also to the bank to withdraw the letters. He felt glad that there were only two more hours before she returned. When he heard the sound of the car entering the garage he went out to meet her, relieved her of her packages and helped her take off her overcoat. It was the first time he had touched her, except for the handshake they had exchanged upon his arrival, and he did it a bit hesitantly, with his fingertips.

"I'm going upstairs to change," said Petra. "Then I'll make lunch. Most of it's already prepared; it'll be ready in ten minutes."

Fabrizio would have liked to volunteer his help, but he was afraid he might just bother her. He watched her as she brought the plates from the kitchen, and only at the end, just to show his willingness, did he make up his mind to carry the chairs to the table.

He intended to ask about the Fritz Oberhofer letters during the meal, but in spite of himself he completely forgot about them as he became absorbed in watching and listening to Petra, seeing her again now after their first, short separation. He felt like someone who by chance happens to attend the solemn rites of an unknown cult and takes great care not to do anything that might be considered improper or sacrilegious.

After lunch Petra said she was going to rest for an hour or so. Fabrizio let her go upstairs first, staying behind in the living room for a few minutes as the house etiquette required. Then he also went up to his room. On the desk, bound together with a white ribbon, was a bundle of letters.

"*Liebchen*," began the first, "it's so dreadful that I should have to wait nearly a month before I can kiss again the fragrant little buttercup you keep between your legs."

There were eighteen letters, dated from May 3 to May 25,

1910. Fritz at the time was getting ready to rejoin his love in Mondsee and wrote to her nearly every day, spicing the accounts of his travel preparations with flights of passionate eroticism. He called her *Liebchen, Mein Kind, Schätzerle*. There were no envelopes. It was therefore impossible to determine the name of the addressee—little matter, thought Fabrizio, what difference could it make?—or the address. Little matter here too, since by now he was positive this was the house.

On the desk, next to the letters, there were photocopies as well, neatly tucked away inside a large brown envelope addressed to him, in Milan. Petra must have done all of this earlier, before his arrival, with the intention of sending him the copies by mail; then perhaps another plan had come into her mind, though Fabrizio refused to wonder what it might have been.

He began to feel overcome by the same inertia that had gripped him after the publication of the biography of Fritz Oberhofer. These last few days he had remained suspended in a kind of half-sleep, not once pricked by impatience as he waited for Monday to come so that Petra could give him the letters. In fact, he had very nearly forgotten about them. He had spent the morning in bed, immersed in a false lethargy, the kind that takes hold of those who pretend to be tired but in fact lack the willpower to start the day. His mortal shell had turned into a slow, viscous slug. He realized that months had passed since he had last made love, gone swimming or even laughed.

And now, even as he reproached himself for all this, he felt an overwhelming aversion to the idea of removing his things from their drawers, packing his suitcase and returning to Milan.

He remembered the resentment he had felt toward his father during the last years of his life, after the bankruptcy. Even death had seemed to him an act of extreme sloth, of indifference to others, of abdication of dignity and duty. He remembered the shuffling footsteps, the odious, everlasting slippers, the lifeless eyes and hunched back that made him seem thirty years older than his sixty years. Though he was not ill he spent almost all of his time in bed, tray on his knees, playing endless games of solitaire, smoking, eating candies. He wouldn't wash, shave, answer letters or make any of the telephone calls necessary to settle the last debts remaining from his financial collapse.

"He does it out of spite," Fabrizio would say.

"It's a disease like any other," Teodora rebutted. "You can't hold it against him."

Now he too was ill, with a disease that was perhaps a form of punishment.

He had always found so many excuses for himself—for his indecision, his fears, his resistance to love, his inner resentments. But did that vast, self-protective mechanism which had an answer for politics, fashion, history, cultural revolutions and collective madness—did it really explain everything? Was there not perhaps a flaw inside his own heart, something that concerned only him, the little man in the corner of the fresco, and had nothing to do with the rest of the wall?

When at fourteen he had gotten so excited at the sight of that flash of pink beneath the dress of Miss Ferzetti—the stern math teacher who had nothing at all seductive about her but still kept that nothing carefully wrapped in modesty, severity and dignity—what, deep down, had agitated him so? Was it not perhaps something perverse, a sign of some inborn depravity? Might not that disproportionate lust have arisen from the very thought of violating another's secret, of penetrating another human being with one's mind—an excitement aroused precisely, and solely, by the knowledge that this other was unwilling? And was this merely an odd sexual quirk—such as most everyone has—or was it the sign of an evil heart?

But all that seemed so remote now. Miss Ferzetti, like Fulvia, the great thuja, the structuralists and the rest, were like images flattened against a distant background. The only thing that seemed real was the altar of shadows, the gap in time into which he had fallen. Yet while he sat at the desk by the window, which for him was the intersection of inside and outside, and hence also a potential time machine that might take him out of that motionless pool and back to the world of change, he knew—oh, how he knew—that he had to escape and that the spell of that house was an evil one.

Petra had gone downstairs and was now making tea. Fabrizio joined her and thanked her for the letters.

"I was thinking of leaving tomorrow, with the photocopies you made for me. In Milan I have all the documentation that I'll need to draw up the notes and an index of names. In the meantime, you could write down some of your memories of your grandmother and tell how these letters came into your hands . . . How *did* you come upon the letters, Fräulein Ebner?"

"Someday I'll let you know. You go ahead with your plans for now."

"Well, eventually we should exchange the work that we've done, ask each other's advice and then perhaps go over everything together . . . We could both be credited as editors of the correspondence when it comes out . . . As for the sharing of the royalties, I'll leave that up to you. We could arrange it so that the German and Italian editions come out at the same time."

Petra waited for him to finish speaking, then nodded as if to indicate that she had understood the meaning of his words. But she said nothing.

And yet it was imperative that she say something. There is a rule that applies to every spell, namely, that it has to be broken by someone from the outside; the person under the spell can never free himself. Fabrizio started talking to the motionless visage, going on and on, more and more feverishly, falteringly, anxious to provoke a response that might liberate him. As she continued to remain silent, he tried to distract her by talking about other things, hoping that by coming back to the subject all of a sudden, he might surprise her into saying something that would release him from a pact, an oath that he did not remember having taken but which was there, between them, as solid as a mass of stone.

He even tried to make her laugh, though she semed not to have laughed since the day when she and her grandmother found nineteen porcini mushrooms all alike. But he alone laughed at his jokes, his humor ringing in his ears with an artificial sound, as coarse and profane as a plastic bag in the middle of a green glade.

For the rest of the afternoon, and then during the evening meal and after, Petra sat in front of him, absolutely calm, hardly ever responding, looking him straight in the face, her features conveying an expression describable only in terms of symmetry and balance.

When she brought him his cognac and climbed the stairs to go to bed, she still had not uttered a single word to set him free, or to deny him his freedom.

AFTER RETURNING TO HIS ROOM Fabrizio did not go to
bed right away, but stayed seated awhile at the desk. He had
left the light off and the shutters open; the full moon was
shining over the lake. The weather had not yet turned cold
enough to freeze the surface, except in a few of the shadier
reaches. The water, enclosed within its ring of white mountains, flickered under the moonlight. Seen from his vantage
point, the lake seemed endless and the band of light that ran
across it was like a path that one could take to go anywhere.
The path extended from the lake, across the shiny desk top,
across the flowery rug and over Fritz and Maria's bed before
stopping at the spines of the books lined up along the wall.

When Fabrizio turned and looked into the room, the
shining path actually seemed to have its source right there,
at the back of the room, issuing from this spot and hence out
the window, stretching all the way to the ends of the earth.

A bit later he followed the band of light toward its point
of origin and went to bed. His mind was already teeming with
the fleeting thoughts of half-sleep.

*   *   *

The moonbeam moved slowly across the room; when it was on the door, the door opened and Petra entered. Without a word she drew near the bed, raised her nightgown over her head, slipped it off and tossed it onto the shining path where it whirled momentarily, suspended in air like a matador's cape.

She slid between the sheets next to Fabrizio and took his face in her hands, kissing it and speaking to him. He could see her lips moving in the half-light; he heard a murmuring sound but could not make out the words because she was pressing his ears so tightly that it deafened him. Fabrizio wrapped his arms around the woman's thin body, and beneath his hands her skin felt cold to the touch and smooth as that of a celluloid doll. He fondled her, searching for a human fold, a point of sensation and warmth that would suggest flesh, viscera and blood beneath that skin; but her breasts seemed to have no nipples, her mons no hair, and her outer shell seemed to hold nothing but lifeless synthetic stuffing—unless perhaps Fabrizio's hands, upon contact with that cold body, had lost their sensation, as if they were wrapped in rubber gloves. He began to feel an inexpressible horror that slowly kept growing until it turned into a kind of resigned arousal, as sometimes happens in dreams when the two things become confused. His arousal ended in a brief moment of pleasure, a jolt, the pain now gone and with it his shame. The woman spoke to him again but with her hands still over his ears. Then she got up from the bed, picked up her nightgown and left the room in silence.

The following morning, on the table, next to Fabrizio's cup, along with the *Courier*, were two Italian newspapers.

"They're from yesterday, unfortunately," said Petra. "It seems hard to believe, with all the modern means of transportation that we have. I'm afraid you'll just have to read the news of your country a little late."

The sound of her voice cast the night they had just spent into the depths of a very distant past, driving it far from the clean white tablecloth and the two polite, formal table companions. Fabrizio answered her in the same tone: "That's all right. I appreciate your kindness."

He skimmed through the newspapers, idly playing with his cup of coffee. He got up from the table and sat down in an armchair, and when the cleaning woman burst in noisily with her vacuum cleaner, he went up to his room to sit at the writing table.

The room had already been put back in order when he was downstairs, otherwise he would have liked to go back to bed. It was a glorious day outside; propped up against the pillows, he would have had the lake spread out before him, closed in on two sides by mountains but boundless, or so it seemed, in the other direction—the very one that started from the bed and went on without end. For over there, where the horizon became a blur of fog, not only did the mountains serving as lateral embankments not join together to dam up that thing called a lake but which secretly was not a lake, they actually took a step aside to line the way for the great main highway as it passed en route to the rest of the world.

If he had not, in the past, read so many medical articles warning against the dangers of overeating, seeing the scourge of malnutrition only in third-world countries and accusing the West of having ruined its own regulatory mechanisms by pushing the meaning of satiety more and more toward excess, he would have thought he was starving to death.

He no longer knew how long he had been eating little or nothing. He felt his pants around him like two empty tubes propped against his shoes, which miraculously carried him the few steps he had to make from the bed to the dining room chair, then from the chair to the armchair. His walk through the snow with Petra a few days before now seemed, in retrospect, a remarkable achievement.

He was dying—of hunger, of bewitchment, of the will to die, of an unknown disease, of very premature old age—he didn't know what. But he was dying.

He had started dying long before, when he went off to look for Fritz Oberhofer in secret, like a thief, shunning the company of the living only to fall, thanks to his cowardice, into a diabolical pact with the world of ghosts. How could he, the Germanist, not have remembered the lessons of German literature, which from Goethe to the fabulists to Chamisso had taught that pacts of this sort always turn out to be terrible bargains?

He dragged through the day in a haze but felt no boredom. Petra did not go to the sawmill. She had taken out some knitting to keep herself busy, something evidently quite easy, for she knitted away without ever looking down at her work, her gaze fixed on him all the while. And although they said very little to each other, their conversation consisting more of pauses than of words, Petra engaged him nonetheless with her silent company.

It was the same in the days that followed. Now that Fabrizio had Fritz Oberhofer's letters, he no longer felt like working on them. Petra had put away the originals, leaving the copies on Fabrizio's desk, and every now and then he would glance at one of them distractedly—but it was always something he would find himself doing almost involuntarily, when, having been chased out of the living room to allow the maid to clean on the two days of the week when she came, he would come back to his room and find the bed made up again. Only in those moments did he still sit at the writing table, and as his gaze no longer soared out over the lake but now fell from his eyes like a tear, coming to rest at times on the letters, it was then that, without wanting to, he would begin to read.

The rhythm of Fabrizio's life was marked by the meals, the only daily event he anticipated and around which he ordered his time, though he hardly ate anything anymore. In the morning when sitting at the lovely breakfast table set in white and silver, he would have only a small cup of black coffee.

Then, when Petra resumed her occasional morning visits to the sawmill, he stopped going downstairs for breakfast; before leaving she would knock on his door and, finding him still immersed in a half-sleep, would leave a Thermos of coffee on the night table. On those days he would stay in bed until one in the afternoon, at which time Petra, having returned, would call him for lunch.

His inertia no longer made him feel in any way uneasy; he felt, on the contrary, as though he had undergone one of those mutations of the species that occur and are destined to endure because they are more suited to the particular environment.

The space around him seemed to contain only things past, completed; missing were all the goals, large and small, that must be attained in a lifetime.

Carrying out an action was like pulling out from time's archives a whole series of actions already filed away inside an immutable order—afterward, all he could do was file it back in the dark cabinets where it belonged, giving up on the idea of ever seeing that action produce even the slightest ripple in the crystalline stillness of the surrounding air.

In other places—such as Milan—the year must have ended right about then, and a new one begun. Fabrizio, who could still appreciate the pleasures of paradox, thought that it must have been Mario himself who, with the extraordinary efficiency of his actions, had effected that change merely by drinking a glass of champagne at midnight and putting on a new shirt the next day.

Two or three days later Petra finished what she had been knitting—a white cardigan, which she donned as soon as she had finished sewing on the buttons. She immediately started working on something else, this time a piece of embroidery that demanded much greater concentration on her part. She applied the tambour to the spot on a pure white piece of linen where she had traced a pattern in indelible pencil; then she opened her box of colored threads, put on her glasses, chose the shades with great care, giving all her attention to the embroidery. She would raise her eyes toward Fabrizio only when she had finished one strand of thread and was about to begin another; in that interval between colors she would bathe him for a moment in the serene light of her gaze. Fabrizio sat in front of her, following the slow emergence of the pattern.

Petra returned often to Fabrizio's room; yet she never went upstairs at the same time as he, and she never opened his door before he had turned off the light and had gotten into bed. Fabrizio would lie there waiting, hiding behind closed eyelids, terror-struck as he heard the faint squeak of the door, pinned against the bed as though hurled to the bottom of a vortex by a bizarre lust that fed on submission and shame.

She was the one who, acting only on arbitrary whim; she was the one who directed their union and who—regardless of their respective anatomies—possessed him and penetrated him to his very soul; and she was the one who decided when to leave without saying a word.

Bit by bit, with each passing night, the figure that entered Fabrizio's room began to acquire specific features. Her body became warmer, the glow of her hair against the dim light of the window took on a golden hue. The name "Petra," drawn from the cold stillness of the mineral realm, and the woman who bore it were like a white page that could be covered with any design imaginable. For this reason, in the daytime when Fabrizio thought back on those nighttime encounters, he tried to etch that name and that woman in his memory. Yet this was an arbitrary simplification, he feared, which he accepted only because of his extreme mental fatigue, for as the traits of his visitor began slowly to emerge they resembled those of Petra less and less. Moreover, those dark moments always remained hermetically sealed off, never upsetting the amazing symmetry of the days, the naked precision of the ritual gestures that filled the motionless space closed within that house. During the day, Petra bore no outward sign of her nighttime visits; her nunnish face remained unruffled, her demeanor as solemn and serene as ever.

More and more often now Petra would go out and leave Fabrizio by himself. The only mornings she stayed home were the two days that the cleaning woman came. Even when she didn't have to go to the sawmill, she still had her religious obligations and her salutary walks to keep herself busy. At times it seemed as though she wanted to test the strength of the chains in which her prisoner was bound. At such moments she would enter his room, placing her black silhouette between him and the white square of the window. To Fabrizio, who lay flat on the bed, the distortion of perspective seemed to transform her into a fir tree: wide and flat at the hem of her skirt, which was at the same level as his eyes, and then gradually narrower toward the waist, past the shoulders, and up to the highest point, the head. The point would say, "Do we feel like going out for a walk today, Herr Garrone?"

"I don't feel up to it," he would answer. "I am very tired."

"Well, then, if you don't need anything, I'm going to go."

"No, no, I don't need anything, Fräulein Ebner."

She began to leave him alone every now and then in the evening as well, when she went to Salzburg to hear music or to see a play. Fabrizio thought she must have resumed her old habits, becoming again the churchgoing busybody, the cultural, social and religious pillar of her community.

But had she also taken advantage . . . of a breach in the fortress? A rent in the fabric of time? A lightninglike blow, swift as a cat's paw—and just like that, a secret intruder had entered the temple of stillness.

Or was there more than one? How many other presences might be floating around that house? Fabrizio realized that it was just as arbitrary to call his inert, supine body "I" as it was to call the white nocturnal visitor it awaited "Petra."

At certain moments he seemed to understand why he had thought of his hostess's mother as the zero factor in the code that bore the family secret. She was the neutral point, the pure point in time, in the succession of generations: lifeless existence, soul without movement, foundry without metal or flame. Without even breaking their seals, she had passed on to Petra both legacies—that of Maria Lettner and that of the zealot from Linz—each of them intact, separate and reinforced for so long in their mutual dissimilarity that they could only be spent one at a time, in accordance with different rites and in different, noncommunicating realms of time, space and mind.

But was it really this way? Where did he come in? What role was he acting out? What had led him to this fatal prison in the first place? He played with these questions for only a very short time, too tired to think of any answers.

Petra would always stay home on the days when the cleaning woman came. She would don an apron and follow her around through her various chores, helping to move Fabrizio from one room to another so that the woman could sweep under his armchair. On those days Fabrizio had to get up early and eat breakfast downstairs while the maid was tidying up the rooms above.

One morning, however, when still in bed after Petra had gone out, he heard the front door open. "Fräulein Ebner?" shouted a voice. "Fräulein Ebner, I tried to call, but I couldn't get the line."

Fabrizio remembered that the telephone had not rung for a long time in that house. This confirmed a lazy suspicion, an idle thought that had been gathering dust in his mind for the last few days: that Petra had disconnected the phone with the express purpose of keeping him even more isolated from the rest of the world. A needless precaution, however; not once had it occurred to him to call anyone. Even if he hadn't

168

felt so overwhelmed by inertia, the idea of contacting Mario's office, Fulvia's apartment or Teodora's penthouse from Petra's house in Mondsee would have been inconceivable; it would have seemed a contradiction of logic, something that would never have worked.

Down there the world went around as usual, the world where everything seemed clear—and therefore *was* clear, since everyone wisely made do with appearance—where everything had its own specific height, width and depth; where the days passed according to the dictates of the calendar, with no accelerations, decelerations or turnabouts allowed; where everything that violated the laws of verisimilitude simply did not exist; any words uttered in Petra's house and directed toward that world would have gotten lost somewhere along the line or else become so distorted as to reach the other end in the form of incomprehensible sounds.

The maid was now climbing the stairs with her heavy step.

"I can't come tomorrow, so I thought I'd get the housework done today. Fräulein Ebner?" she repeated. She knocked on Petra's door.

"She's gone out," shouted Fabrizio. "I'm the only one here."

The woman took a few more steps and stopped in front of his door.

"May I come in?"

"Please."

"Still in bed? Do you feel ill?"

"I'm tired."

"See what happens to those who don't work by the light of the Good Lord! Always up late ruining your eyes with those books!"

Fabrizio did not have the courage to admit he had done nothing for months and that his weakness was entirely without justification. According to the moral code by which he had been brought up, sloth was the blackest of sins; the woman now scrutinizing him spoke the same language as the most energetic of his governesses, and though she might not have been quite as impeccable in appearance, she had that same fullness of proportion, that same bright gleam in the eye.

"I hadn't realized what time it was," he said. "I'll get up at once, so you can do the room."

"That's the spirit. Go take a little walk. The postman has already come with your newspapers, but let them sit for now. First go outside and get a breath of fresh air."

"All right," he replied, realizing that no actions were, as he had believed, beyond his capacity in and of themselves. It was just that when faced with two alternatives, he could never refrain from choosing the easier one. Obeying, at that moment, required less effort than finding an excuse for his idleness.

─────── 20 ───────

THE MOMENT HE STEPPED OUTSIDE, Fabrizio suffered an attack of dizziness and had to lean against the garden fence. Then it passed, and he began to walk slowly toward the lake. The sky was clear, the air cold and dry. Faraway sounds reached his ears from across the silence, separate and distinct. Only the mountaintops were still white; winter had come and gone without his noticing. A few days after his arrival in Mondsee he had walked with Petra through the first snow; now the last of it had withdrawn to the mountains and the lowland was aglow with the year's first green.

The house disappeared behind him, hidden by a row of trees. A fragrance of wet grass and freshly plowed earth filled him with a forlorn nostalgia, like images out of someone else's past, which he was not allowed to contemplate. And yet it could have been his, all of it—the shade of the plane tree, the cool white wine, the goats frolicking amid the bushes, the bright blue of the Aegean; life had offered this and more, to him as to everyone else. All he had to do was to hold out his hand and say the word and the gift would have been his.

Fabrizio crossed a grassy clearing and continued down a path through the trees. The buds of the deciduous trees shone bright against the black of the evergreens.

"It's like when you receive a parcel," he said to himself. "Though it's addressed to you, it will never be yours unless you open the door for the postman and sign the register."

Why had he never dared? What was he afraid of? That it would just turn out to be a big joke? Maybe, or something like that. No matter what the situation, he never really understood just *how* he should act; all he knew for certain was that whatever choice he made, it would be the wrong one and he would make a fool of himself.

And so he had just stood there, paralyzed by awkwardness, while fate's opportunities passed right by him and into the waiting arms of others. He had reached the height of disgrace and folly when he stopped responding to the smile of a woman like Fulvia, preferring to summon forth a ghost to keep him company.

It had been an ill-fated choice, and a clumsy one too, like pressing the wrong button on a sensitive machine. For from that point on, everything had gone awry, blurring all together in an unending vortex that kept dragging him farther and farther down.

First there was the birth of Maria Lettner, an imaginary character invented by Fabrizio Garrone; then came the real Maria Lettner and all her photographs, greeting cards and the locket with a tuft of her white hair inside. But was it really like that? Was the second Maria born a few months after the first or a hundred years before? And Petra Ebner, that abstract image, geometric figure, composite of perspectives—when was she born and what did she have to do with the woman who came to him at night? History had it that sometime between 1940 and 1944 a little girl entered the world (and in due course came her first little tooth, then school, measles, etc.—a rather stiff creature, not very pretty, but all in all a little girl like all the rest). Then what happened? Was it once again

Fabrizio Garrone the alchemist who, as though wanting to restore the equilibrium between two worlds, a balance upset by the illicit materialization of Maria Lettner's ghost, had this time turned a real woman into a ghost? Or was he nothing more than a powerless onlooker caught between Maria and Petra as they exchanged roles, the one entering inside the other and vice versa? And who was leading the dance, the terrible quadrille of Fabrizio, Fritz, Maria and Petra, absurd, motley cast that they were—a living man, a dead man, a woman who had never existed and a bodiless image—?

Did he have the power to end this game and walk away?

The world around him, so fresh and new, awakened the hope that this might be the morning to make his attempt, to try to return among the living, taking with him something he had learned . . .

Petra suddenly appeared around a bend in the path through the trees. The cold air had placed a veil of color across her meaningless face. She was wearing masculine-looking shoes with rubber soles and a black lamb's-wool overcoat. Everything else about her, thought Fabrizio, could only be described in negatives: she had no beauty, tenderness or cheer—and certainly no faith. She was a pious hypocrite who had found a way to amuse herself a little without having to relinquish the safety of her dusty old rules. She came up alongside Fabrizio and directed both their steps toward home.

"Lovely morning for a walk. What made you decide to go outside?" She was not upset, just politely curious.

"The cleaning woman came and I didn't want to get in her way . . . It was her idea that I should go out for a walk. Sometimes a little push is all you need to overcome laziness . . . Before I knew it, I was already outside."

"But today is Thursday. For the last thirty years Frau Leitnerbrau has always come on Friday."

"Yes, I know. She said she had tried to call to let you know, but the line was down."

"That doesn't surprise me." She made a gesture with her hand toward one of the mountains facing the lake. "She lives in a little town behind that bluff, a thousand meters up. Their telephone service is a bit primitive."

As he walked beside the woman, keeping pace with her wooden steps and engaging her in conversation, he felt himself invaded throughout by the wonderful sensation of relief one feels upon awakening from a nightmare. The house, when it appeared before him, looked like an old, well-kept structure, nicely proportioned but a bit uninviting. They crossed the flowerless garden and entered the living room.

"Lunch will be ready in half an hour," said Petra.

"I'm going up to my room to look at the papers. Frau Leitnerbrau had me out the door before I could even open them."

He sat down at the window and opened the *Corriere della Sera*. On page three there was an interview with an illustrious scholar of German literature who talked about his forthcoming study. In this study he claimed to have proved, on the basis of precise historical and philological evidence, that *Das Haus am Mondsee* was written not by Fritz Oberhofer but by Maria Lettner. Fritz apparently had recounted to his mistress the story of his first love; Maria then took this account and made a novel out of it, signing it with his name to honor his memory, as he had died in the interim. Thus, with only the four insignificant novels of his youth to fall back on, the writer that Fabrizio thought he had resurrected suddenly vanished from literary history, his place now taken by Maria, one of the few women writers of the German language of any period, and perhaps the only truly great one. The article featured a photograph of her, a serene smile on her face. She had reduced Fritz to the same status as the doctor from Linz, or worse yet, to that of the nameless officer who died at Cassino during the Second World War. That smile seemed, even then, to contain the certainty that, with her real existence protected and reinforced by the invincible authority of common opinion, she would be the one to have the last word.

Of course the letters alone—Fabrizio let his gaze fall on the brown envelope—would be enough to reestablish the truth. Whoever wrote them, signed them "Fritz" and addressed them to a woman waiting for him at Moon Lake was also the author of *Das Haus am Mondsee*, beyond any doubt . . .

Beyond any doubt? But was anything really beyond any doubt? Was credibility a property of objective facts or merely of the people who upheld them? What were Fritz's letters worth in Fabrizio's hands?

The truth of the matter was that Fritz had gotten what was coming to him, and now it was his turn.

The woman who had never existed had finished off the dead writer; now the current extensions of both were in that house, face to face, two tentacles reaching all the way into the present. Fabrizio looked at himself in the mirror above the chest of drawers; some tentacle! He was nothing more than a limp, transparent excrescence already cut off at the root, the pathetic specimen of an extinct breed, who spoke in a dead language. At the very moment in which he had deluded himself into thinking he could collect his forces, this sudden, scornful counterthrust had flattened him before he could even stand up to fight.

And yet he wanted with all his heart to escape, to break out of that game of mirrors in which he had so unwisely taken delight. Let the dead work it out among themselves, as long as he, Fabrizio Garrone, thirty-eight years old and alive, could make it home with his hide intact. Unreality was not, after all, the peaceful cloister of transparent serenity that he had thought; even in bright, empty spaces hidden dangers lurked and, worse yet, there was no place to take cover. Oh, if only he could reach the other shore, with all its tangled underbrush!

When he went downstairs, Petra was standing in the living room, facing the window that looked over the lake. She seemed

175

not to hear him. She remained completely motionless, as though cut out of black paper and set against the window's bright frame.

"Fräulein Ebner."

The paper-doll figure rippled for a moment as Petra made a half-turn to face him, then settled back into its previous form, a two-dimensional, featureless silhouette.

"Yes?"

"I'm going to leave on tonight's flight out. It has been an enchanting stay and I am very grateful to you for having me. But, as I'm sure you understand, I really must go home now and get back to my work."

Petra, without answering him, sat down at the table and with a slight nod invited Fabrizio to do the same. She did not change the subject, not deigning to make any attempt whatsoever to steer the conversation. She merely remained silent for a few minutes while his words, which had already washed off her back like water on a swan's feathers, faded into nothingness, down to their last echo.

Only when the time for answers, protests and excuses was well past did Petra finally speak: "I hope you didn't wear yourself out this morning."

Fabrizio did in fact feel quite tired, drunk with fresh air, and now he felt as if he had wasted his last reserves of strength trying to communicate his intentions.

"I'm a little tired," he admitted. "After lunch I think I'll go rest awhile."

As they ate, exchanging comments on the splendor of the unusually early spring, Fabrizio once again felt the growing, desperate conviction that he would never be able to leave that house until he had somehow made Petra say the words that would set him free.

His only hope was to repeat that he intended to go back to Milan; but this time he had to select the right moment and use the right tone of voice, so that she would have no choice but to acknowledge what he'd said and answer him.

But even as he was formulating this thought he knew that Petra Ebner would never let herself be forced to do anything; her imperturbability was without breach.

They were finishing their meal when suddenly they heard the doorbell ring. Fabrizio looked out the window that gave onto the yard.

At the end of the little footpath, outside of the gate—dressed all in Gucci, Pringle of Scotland and Harris tweed—stood the little warrior angel, her golden hair radiant in the spring sun. Her sky-blue Fiat was parked on the other side of the road. Petra's gaze followed Fabrizio's and, after crossing an incalculable distance, came to rest on Fulvia.

"A woman," she said.

"Fulvia," whispered Fabrizio.

"I beg your pardon?"

Fabrizio got up from his chair and started for the door.

"I'll go see who it is," said Petra.

He hesitated a moment as the woman went out onto the footpath, closing the black wooden door behind her. Changing direction, Fabrizio took a few faltering steps toward the window. His eyes fixed themselves on the sunlit figure waiting outside the gate.

Fulvia who stood in line at the post office to pay the registration fee on her car. Fulvia who would come out of the grocery store with plastic bags full of food. Fulvia who would slip off her sweater, lifting her lovely arms high over her head. Fulvia who sunbathed on a rock by the sea. Fulvia who stirred risotto with a wooden spoon. Fulvia with her harmonious movements, Fulvia with her talent for life, Fulvia friend to things and people.

Fulvia, who in the last twenty-four hours had read the article in the *Corriere*, had decided to open the two packets he had sent to her, and now had come to take him home.

"Home, home." Home?

Fabrizio sighed. His heart filled again with a desperate nostalgia for a memory that wasn't his, for something that had no part in his unraveled existence strewn across vast empty spaces full of darkness; what he wanted could only belong to small compact lives full of conviction, boldly poised toward the future like a fresh April morning. Oh, if only, if only . . .

If only he could have looked ahead (but where?) instead of around himself. If only he could not see the millions of plastic bags produced every day and subjected to a very brief tryout (the half hour it took to get home from the supermarket) before being immediately sent off to fulfill their true purpose: to cover the earth, to float on the sea, to taint the atmosphere with their poisonous fumes; not see the kids with ears sandwiched between those dreadful headsets, trapped in a solitude beyond reach, where only bad music mattered; not see the torrid Christmases and freezing Julys amid the sinister hums of heaters and air conditioners; not see the obscene greed that turns everything into vice, into drugs: suntans, athletics, work, television, food—all of them drugs—even diets, even fasting a form of greed; not see the formula that held the whole mad system together, that warped time into grotesque shapes like a three-thousand-dollar bonsai tree, with the past unanimously viewed as through a fish's eye, flat as a shadow on the wall (Brecht and Sophocles, two classics roughly contemporary with each other), and the present inflated and overrated like an insufferable little jerk, an obnoxious, spoiled child whose every whim is anticipated, whose every word and gesture is trumpeted to the four winds. And, between past and present, a little strip of time for minor revivals.

If only he could not see it all, or else have the guts to keep his distance, proud as a pillar saint high above the desert of garbage and blather.

If only if only . . .

But how could he? From the little Fiat's sky-blue roof the sun sent flashes of light that foreboded the color and shine of jukeboxes, miniature golf courses and summer swimming pools.

Her hand resting on the little gate, Petra answered the Italian woman's questions. They communicated mostly through gestures, but seemed to understand each other perfectly. Petra nodded, smiled and then shook her head. She made a gesture with her hand as if to say "a long time ago." Yes, he did come here, but he left a long time ago. He went back to Milan. More than that I don't know. *Es tut mir Leid.* Her hand returned to its resting place on the little gate with a gentle, graceful movement.

Fulvia asked a few more questions, then thanked the woman and walked back to her car. As she opened the door, she turned around toward the house, as if seized by a moment of doubt, of hesitation. But her good sense prevailed. In this world some things were possible, the rest impossible, and the one that had flashed through her mind at that moment was impossible.

The sky-blue Fiat started back for Milan.

"A tourist who lost her way," said Petra when she returned.

Fabrizio sat at his window and looked out at the watery road that would never take him anywhere. He now realized that he too, in the end, had received an inheritance of his own, something that had retained its value, its power, after everything else had lost meaning; something that had brought him to this house and would keep him here to the end. Now that he knew what his legacy was, he would accept it without resistance and spend it all, until nothing was left. The rite of his extinction would be performed solemnly and in full awareness.

His mind flitted about for a moment, then came to rest a short distance away.

"I should draw up a will," he thought. But this immediately seemed like far too difficult a task, something that would only create needless complications. Teodora was his only legal heir, and he could count on her to distribute his spoils fairly.

179

She would collect his royalties and set aside, for herself and for each of her children, a few small objects of little value to be kept as mementos.

She would not forget Fulvia; to her she would bequeath a piece of furniture or a painting—Fabrizio didn't quite know what, except that it would be the right thing. Even in terms of its worth: valuable enough to express her thanks for what she had tried to do for her brother but not so precious as to oblige her to wear the widow's weeds a second time. Teodora did not like waste. Fulvia was pretty, lively, warm and generous; she should forget as quickly as possible and start over again . . . Naturally the Saint Jerome, the books and all the other things to which Fabrizio was most attached would go to Mario. "The election lights on Fortinbras . . ." his lips murmured as his gaze went out across the lake together with something that was flying away, vanishing past the mountains. "The election lights on Fortinbras . . ."

He could almost see Teodora crossing the street, the painting wrapped up and tucked under her arm. She looked pale, shaken. Mario also looked shaken as he opened the door to let her into his house. But there would be no tearful scenes.

"I want you to have this."

"Are you sure?"

"Of course I'm sure."

"Thank you. I'd be glad to have it."

"I'd also like you to have the books, the desk . . . Send a couple of porters for everything later."

Not to mention the two most precious bequests, who would probably inherit each other. Fulvia would have Mario and Mario Fulvia. The thought neither saddened nor consoled Fabrizio. It stayed in his mind for just a brief moment, seeming not to refer to any sort of possible future but to something that had already happened in a very distant past.

Fabrizio lay sunken in his bed. Petra placed her black fir-tree silhouette between him and the window.

"I was thinking of going out for a walk," she said. "Would you like to join me?"

"I don't think so. I'm very tired."

"Can I get you anything?"

"No, thank you. Everything's fine."

Petra descended the stairs, took her gloves from the shelf and stepped out onto the sunlit path.